BLOOD MOON

THE SEARCHERS
BOOK TWO

JESSICA MARTING

SHADOW PRESS

BLOOD MOON

Blood Moon (The Searchers Book 2)

ISBN 978-1-989780-26-8

Second Edition

This book was originally published by Evernight Publishing with the title *Dark Moon*. It was been revised, expanded, and re-edited.

Cover art by German Creative

For David.

CHAPTER

ONE

4 May 1889
Dresden, Germany

D*ear Edgar,*
     You might find this unbelievable, but I'm bringing back a friend with me to New York. His name is Max Sterling and I expect you to be nice to him. Also, please ask Frank and Beth to be ready for his arrival. He will share my room. Please do not be scandalized. (Ha! As if anyone in the Burgess family could possibly be scandalized!) I've already sent them a letter telling them we will arrive at the New York City Airfield on the 30th of May on the Carl Friedrich Gauss *at six in the evening. Please be there to collect us.*

     I am sure you and the New York branch of the Searchers received my cables and letters about the "problems" I discovered whilst in Europe (whilst! Max's high English ways are rubbing off on me!). Me and Max have taken care of a great deal of those problems and are enjoying a peaceful stay in Dresden right now. He is very excited to meet you and our family once we reach New York. Edgar, for the first time in my life, I am in love. We saved each other's lives. I will tell you all about it when we come home.

1

Also, I received your cable about the disappearance of Molly McKillip. I'm so sorry to hear of that, Edgar. I know how special she was to you. We will talk about her further once me and Max land in America.

Much love to you always,
Your irritating sister, Ada

~

IT WAS INCREDIBLY SATISFYING to come across a den of sleeping vampires. It made Edgar Burgess's job that much easier, and, frankly, staking them while they slept was much safer. The bloodsucking persuasion was strong enough to slow down even the most determined monster hunter, and Edgar could swear they were getting smarter, too.

Or maybe Edgar was getting dumber, or more reckless as he got older and had fewer things in life to care about. His brother and sister had suggested that a few times. It was a possibility Edgar didn't want to think about too much.

He expertly staked the vampire curled on its side, slumbering on the cellar's dirt floor. The crumbling tenement the vampire nest had taken up in had been abandoned after a fire ripped through its upper floors in the summer of 1886, nearly three years' prior.

The cellar was filthy enough that Edgar could leave behind the greasy piles of ash they disintegrated into after staking. The curled-up vampire gave a final gurgle in its sleep before crumbling into dust, leaving only its clothes behind. Edgar nudged the dirty garments out of the ash, and with his gloved hand, picked them up and flung them into a corner with the rest of the vampires' clothing. He'd already staked a female and two males, with one more of the latter to go.

Edgar swung his lantern over the cellar, finding the last vampire sprawled on top of a battered, oversized steamer trunk that could probably double as a coffin. *A smart vampire would have slept* inside *the trunk,* Edgar thought. He raised his stake and mallet and plunged it into the monster's chest, spraying oily ash all over the trunk and himself.

"Damn," he muttered. Thank God his overcoat was a dark color, otherwise he'd never get the stains out. He wiped a few beads of sweat off his brow, noting with disgust that his gloved fingertips came away streaked with gray.

He pushed the vampire's clothing off the trunk, coughing at the ash whirling in the air. "Damn again. That must have been an older one." Undead beings tended to be dustier with age once they were finally killed for good.

His head had stopped aching once the vampires were dead, and he couldn't sense any more left in the derelict building. Of course, that didn't mean there weren't any more out there. New York always had a vampire problem, and the question was how bad it was at any given time. But the daytime meant Edgar could slip out of the cellar to the street, where Brooklyn was already waking up, and return home. He could rest for a few hours, then pick up some work at the Coney Island Airfield. They always needed some extra help with its construction, and he would be glad to receive the money. He'd been spending these last weeks hunting vampires on his own time.

His heart squeezed painfully when he thought about why he was rushing headlong into solo vampire hunting. It was a combination of regret and fear. He didn't know which made him more selfish: that he hadn't told Molly he loved her a long time ago, or that the night she had been spirited away by a vampire, he'd passed off his headache—a telltale sign of a nearby vampire—as another symptom of the cold he'd come down with after falling into the Hudson River during a particularly difficult hunt.

Dismissing the headache, he decided. It shouldn't even be a question which was worse. If not for him and his laziness that night, Molly wouldn't have been taken. She mattered above all else.

A scratching sound from the inside of the steamer trunk had him turning around. Was a cat trapped in there? Vampires had been known to eat animals when humans were scarce, or it was too dangerous to hunt them.

He rapped on the trunk's top, vampire ashes falling to the scarred lid. "Meow?" he said, then immediately felt like an idiot.

The scratching turned into a rapid pounding against the lid, followed by a muffled but very human yelp. "Is someone there? Let me out! Please!"

Could it be...? Edgar's pulse sped up at the possibility.

"Shit!" He knew whoever was in there wasn't a vampire; they all passed out at dawn, a compulsion none could disobey. He fumbled with the latches on the trunk and found it locked. "Just a minute."

"Please help me!" The voice was female, familiar to him, and now sobbed softly. Or he could just be imagining that familiarity out of desperation and guilt. Either way, he had to help her out.

Edgar gave up with fumbling with the trunk's

latch. He popped it off with his stake and mallet, then flipped open the lid. A blonde head popped up, and he stepped back in surprise and relief as he recognized the trunk's occupant. "Molly! My God!"

She had lost weight since he saw her last. Her hair was matted, and dried blood was crusted to her dirty dress and exposed skin. There was a lot of it, considering how shredded her clothing was. But it was Molly McKillip, recently disappeared young widow, and his neighbor.

She greedily sucked in deep breaths of dusty air before her gaze fixated on Edgar's face. Shock spread across her features. "Edgar?" she whispered. Her eyes were wide and frightened.

His heart thundered against his ribs. He blinked a couple of times, as if to make sure she was real. "Molly," he said, reaching for her, but she shrank back, eyeing the mallet and stake in his hands.

Molly McKillip wouldn't have known about the existence of vampires before she ended up in this abandoned tenement cellar, let alone that her next-door neighbor was a vampire hunter.

She licked her dry, cracked lips. "What the hell are you? Are you one of *them*?" Her voice was soft, but Edgar heard the tremor of fear in it.

He laid down his stake and mallet, holding up his hands in mock surrender. "No. I kill them."

She looked around the cellar. "Where are they?"

Edgar nodded his head toward the pile of ash and garments. "Over there. I staked them when the sun came up."

"So it's morning?"

He nodded.

She choked back a sob and rubbed her teary eyes with dirty hands. She opened her mouth, then closed it, as if deciding which question to ask first. "Did you come to save me?"

Yes! he wanted to shout. *I've been looking for you in every nest for weeks, my kill rate is the highest of the Searchers' New York branch, maybe even the entire east coast, and I'm doing this because I love you more than I could ever tell you and it was my fault you were kidnapped!*

But he didn't. Instead, he replied simply, "Yes." He held out his hands. "Let me help you out of there."

"Did you kill Agate, too?"

Edgar dropped his hands and looked at the pile of clothes in the corner. "I don't know. I staked five today. I don't look for identifying information before staking them."

"Is that what those sounds were? I didn't know." She looked at the scene before them, at the filthy clothes and dust spilling out of them, and shuddered. A wooden stake slammed into a vampire's heart made a very distinctive, wet sound, reminiscent of the noises made by meat being butchered. Edgar was used to it, although he supposed the noises would be disconcerting to someone unfamiliar with them.

"Agate always wore a black overcoat, even though it's getting warmer," she said. Her eyes took on a faraway look as she recalled his appearance.

"A lot of vampires wear black. I think they think it adds to the effect."

"He has light hair, almost white," she said. "He went, um, naked quite a bit, too. Did you kill him?"

Her eyes were hopeful, and Edgar hated to break her heart. He would have remembered a white-haired, naked vampire, and there was none in his list of kills this morning. "I don't think so," he said. Her face fell, and a tear slid down one grimy cheek. He stripped off his dirty gloves and shoved them in his trouser pocket, holding his hands out to her again. "Let me help you up."

Her face was wary and eyes glassy, and she hesitated for a second before letting him lift her out of the steamer trunk. She was lighter than she should be, delicate as a bird.

She swayed on her feet, and Edgar steadied her. "Do you think you can walk?" he asked.

Molly nodded and dragged a hand across her eyes, tears smearing the dirt and blood caked on her skin. "Yes."

He took in her filthy, torn dress and disheveled hair and knew they wouldn't be able to get out of the cellar and to the streets without attracting attention. He shucked off his overcoat and draped it around her shoulders. "Let's get out of here," he said.

She stuck her arms in the coat and wrapped it around herself. It was comically oversized, but she didn't seem to care. "Ed, what happened to them?"

"I killed them," he repeated. He would reassure her of their deaths every hour if he had to, if doing so would put her mind at ease. May as well be honest, since she knew about vampires' existence. "I'm a vampire hunter. My entire family is. We're called Searchers."

Confusion shadowed her features. "I mean, what happened to them to become vampires?"

"They're created by exchanging blood with humans. It's irreversible. Once someone is a vampire, they can never go back to being human." There were rare cases of humans and vampires co-existing. Such a partnership was the reason the Burgess family had the vampire-detecting abilities they did, thanks to dhampir ancestors.

She was quiet for a few seconds, absorbing these new details. "I thought you worked at the Brooklyn Airfield," she said. Her voice had taken on a fractured quality, her eyes still a little glazed, as if her mind and body weren't working in sync. She'd latched on to the one thing she knew for certain about him, that he picked up construction work. Something tangible and normal in the human world.

"Coney Island Airfield, and I do that on the side to pick up some extra money. It turns out that staking vampires isn't a great way to earn a living." He looked around the dank cellar again, at the piles of vampire corpses. He didn't trust the building above not to fall down around their ears. "Molly, let's go."

Despite the urgency in his tone, she stayed rooted to the dirt floor, taking in her surroundings in the dim light offered by Edgar's lantern. She was no doubt seeing the cellar in a different light. "They fed from me," she said, fresh tears spilling down her cheeks.

Pain lodged itself in Edgar's chest at what she must have endured. The puncture marks on her neck and arms hadn't escaped his notice. "I know."

"What do I do now?" she said.

"You come with me," Edgar said. "You know Francis and Elizabeth—my brother and his wife. We're all going to help you. You don't have to re-built your life on your own if you don't want to."

"Do I still have my room?" she asked anxiously.

Molly had rented a room in the house next to

the one the Burgess family shared, and Edgar knew the landlady had long ago thrown away her belongings after she disappeared. There would be no sugar-coating that unfortunate truth. Edgar had spotted her belongings on the street one evening before work, recognizing a few things and saving them for her. "No."

A wordless sob wracked her entire body, thin shoulders shaking under his coat. She let Edgar put his hand on the small of her back and guide her out of the abandoned tenement, to the street where Brooklyn was waking up.

Molly leaned against Edgar Burgess as he led her out of the cellar to the street, where she saw dawn breaking for the first time in weeks. How long had she been gone? She stopped keeping track of the days and nights after the first couple of sleepless days in the trunk, but there had still been a bite in the air the night she was tricked into leaving her home. It wasn't quite warm yet, but the ground was free of snow and the trees were starting to bud. Just how much of her life had she lost?

"What day is it?" she asked.

"The twelfth of May."

Dear God. "Oh, no," she said, a fresh wave of distress washing over her. Her rent was due twice a week, and according to Edgar she had already been evicted.

Her room was gone, and with it, her belongings. Her job at the telegraph office was almost certainly filled by someone else, too. Molly had been living hand-to-mouth since she was widowed three years prior and moved to Brooklyn. Now she was destitute.

Edgar stopped, the shadow of the abandoned tenement behind them. Its upper floors were fire-damaged, and she wished she could finish what the flames had started.

"Molly," he said urgently. "Please believe me when I tell you that you're not going to be alone in this. The Searchers will help you get back on your feet. *I* will help you."

Molly forced herself to meet his gaze, to let herself by reassured by his promises. *He isn't a vampire. You can look him in the eye and know he won't use a mind trick to make you do something.* Still, it was difficult, even when all that looked back at her was a pair of concerned dark eyes, wholly human. There wasn't a reddish tint to them, a telltale sign of vampirism. She didn't feel a pull from looking at him or feel drugged the way she did with the monsters back in the cellar.

He hailed a steam cab that ambled along the street. He ushered her into the backseat and spoke quickly with the driver, giving him the Burgess family's address a couple of miles away before sliding into the backseat next to her.

The steam cab was dirty and reeked of tobacco and vomit, the odor made worse by the pipe being smoked by the driver. The seat was stained and torn, and the section of Brooklyn they were traveling through wasn't particularly safe even during the day. Edgar wore an uncharacteristic look of concern on his face instead of his usual impish, devil-may-care expression that Molly secretly found attractive before she was kidnapped. The seriousness of his expression only underscored how dire her situation was.

"Thank you," she said softly.

He didn't ask for further clarification, only nodded. "It's my job."

"I wish I could repay you in some way," she said.

"There's no need for that. The first thing we're going to do is take you home. Then I'll have to write a report for the Searchers and deliver it to headquarters."

And then what? Molly knew that the Burgess family and this mysterious Searcher organization he kept talking about couldn't care for her indefinitely. She had been barely making do before she was kidnapped, and it had been hard enough to start over with the few measly dollars she had when she resettled in the grittier part of Brooklyn after her husband died. Now she had nothing.

Not wanting to continue wallowing in her own pity party yet, she instead leaned back against the steam cab's grimy seat, waiting to be brought back to the Burgess home.

THE ROW of narrow townhouses was exactly as Molly had imagined it, and she had never seen a better sight in her life. Well, not quite. She stole a glance at Edgar, whose gaze was already pinned on her, gauging her reaction. There was kindness in his dark eyes that sent a corresponding warmth through her body. When was the last time someone had cared for her like this?

Seeing Edgar Burgess when he opened that trunk, and her realization that he hadn't turned into one of *them*, was the best thing she had ever seen. The row houses were second best. Before she could let herself out of the cab, Edgar had already left the backseat and had opened her door for her. It creaked on unoiled hinges. When was the last time anyone had opened a door for her, helped her down to the street?

It had been Edgar, she recalled. She remembered the day she moved into Mrs. Stapleton's boarding house, two years ago. Edgar had happened to be returning home as she arrived and he offered to carry her trunk into the house. Mrs. Stapleton's nod of encouragement at Edgar had told Molly that the man who lived next door was safe.

Now, he guided her up the steep stairs to the front door and let himself in. "Frank! Beth! Look who I found!"

"Coming!" called a familiar woman's voice from upstairs. Footsteps sounded above them, then clattered down the wooden staircase. Frank and Beth Burgess stopped at the foot of the stairs and stared in shock at the sight in the foyer. Beth's next words came out in a breathless whisper. "Molly? Oh, my God!"

"I found her in one of the buildings that burned down a few years ago," Edgar said. "Routine vampire stakings. She was in a trunk."

Only now did Molly remember that she must look as bad as she felt, with her torn clothes, matted hair, and every part of her bearing bloodstains and bite marks. She started to shrug out of Edgar's coat, but he stopped her and helped her out of it, draping it over one arm. "Sorry," he said. "I forgot my manners."

Manners? What did manners matter anymore? "No need to apologize."

Before she could contemplate what she was going to do next, Beth spoke. "I'll get you something to eat right away." She turned to Francis. "Fill up the bathtub in the kitchen," she said briskly. "I'll get some soap and something for her to change into. Molly, how are you otherwise injured?"

Aside from being kept as a living meal for these last weeks, she wasn't. "I'm not."

"I can tell from the look of you that you've lost a great deal of blood," Beth said. "Edgar, be a lamb and run to the butcher shop for some cow's blood. The shop should be open soon. Frank, go to headquarters and tell them what's happened. Bring the doctor back with you." Her tone brooked no argument. She turned back to Molly. "It's important to replace the blood you've lost. Cow's tastes vile, of course, but it's necessary."

Ugh. Molly only nodded, however. She wasn't going to turn away help from people who knew what they were doing, even if meant sucking down blood like a vampire.

While Frank dragged a battered tub into the kitchen and dumped buckets of water in it, Beth put together a meal of leftovers and served it to her in the parlor, apologizing for the lack of fresh food.

Molly didn't care about that, nor did she worry that she descended on the plate like an animal. "I think this is the best meal I've ever eaten," she said. The cold potatoes and slices of boiled beef were absolutely heavenly, and gone in a few minutes.

Beth cleared the plate and brought Molly upstairs, taking her aside in the bedroom she shared with her husband. Her green eyes were serious, her voice quiet.

"I know you've been fed upon," she said. "But I need to know if anything else happened."

Molly knew what "anything else" referred to.

Her stomach turned over the idea, her meal threatening to come back up. "No," she said. Catching Beth's dubious look, she continued. "Nothing else… untoward happened to me, if that's what you're asking. Agate and the others used mind tricks on me and, um, ate from my neck quite a lot, but that was it."

Agate was still out there, somewhere. Molly could never forget that.

Beth's expression was still full of concern. "Are you certain?"

Molly appreciated the other woman's caution. "Yes. They always seemed to prefer their own kind to humans, anyway."

Beth visibly relaxed a little. "That's rarely the case, unfortunately. So I'm relieved to hear that." She crossed the room and opened a battered wooden wardrobe, removing a simple blue dress similar to the one she already wore. She held it out to Molly. "Take this. We don't have much here, but we can certainly outfit you with some clothing."

Molly's heart sank at the confirmation that all her things were really gone. She accepted the dress, draping it over her arm. "Mrs. Stapleton must have tossed everything into the street."

"Not quite, but they're mostly gone," Beth said, regret in her voice. "Edgar saved some of your things. When he gets back from the butcher's, he can get them for you."

Edgar held on to her belongings? Irrational hope flared in Molly, bright as a flame, that he might have known what to save. He'd known to look in that burned-out tenement to find vampires, hadn't he?

Beth continued. "The Searchers won't let you go hungry or without a roof over your head, Molly.

You're one of the few people who've been kidnapped and turned up alive weeks later. That's very rare." She pulled out a couple of blouses, a skirt, and a pair of sturdy trousers from the wardrobe. "I won't have much use for them soon," Beth said, catching Molly's wide-eyed look at her generosity. She dropped her voice to a whisper. "We've only recently found out that I'm expecting. Sometime in the fall, we think."

Something inside Molly warmed at that piece of news. Beth's pregnancy was a ray of light in an otherwise miserable situation. A twinge of longing flared through her; she'd always dreamed of having children of her own. "Congratulations!"

Beth beamed. "Thank you. We're very excited, and we're looking forward to telling Ada when she gets back from Europe."

Molly remembered Edgar's younger sister. Adaline Burgess was just as forthright as her brothers, just as strong as they were. She remembered Edgar's earlier words about their family's line of business. "I suppose she's a vampire hunter, too?"

Beth nodded and led Molly out of the room. "All the Burgesses have the sense. So does my family. We're all Searchers."

"The sense?"

Beth sucked in a small breath, as if she just realized she'd revealed something she shouldn't. She paused at the foot of the stairs, thinking for a few seconds. "It's going to come out sooner or later. We're all descended from dhampirs." Catching Molly's quizzical look, she continued, "Half-vampire, half-human hybrids."

Edgar and Ada were descended from those *things* that had fed from her? Disgust curled low in Molly's belly, and Beth must have noticed, because she immediately tried to clarify what she meant. "They aren't monsters themselves," she said. "Some of their ancestors were. They can sense nearby vampires. So can I, though not as well as Frank or Edgar or Ada." She offered Molly a small smile. "It's a useful talent to have."

"Of course." Still, Molly couldn't keep herself from shuddering a little in revulsion, nor could she keep herself from asking another question. "Are there many dhampirs running around now?"

She followed Beth out of the room and down the stairs. "Doubtful," Beth said over her shoulder. "It's not impossible, but we're much more connected than we used to be even only twenty or thirty years ago. It would be much harder for a dhampir to hide without someone knowing. The Searchers have branches all over the world and the means for faster communication."

"What about vampires?" Molly asked. "How many of them are there?"

They walked into the kitchen, where Francis was still heaving buckets of water into a dented tub. "I think this is as hot as it's going to get," he said, his voice apologetic. "I have a fire going and there are a couple pails of hot water in there, but…"

Bless him, if he thought this wasn't good enough for Molly. "It's perfect. I appreciate this, I really do."

"Let me get some more," Francis said, but Molly stopped him.

"There's enough in there for me to get clean," she said. Catching Francis's dubious expression, she added, "This is plenty. Thank you."

"Are you sure?"

"I am."

"Frank, the lady wants to take a bath for the first time in weeks," Beth said. "She's being polite. Get out." But despite her harsh words, there was a smile on her face as she looked at her husband, and there was a nearly tangible spark in the air when their eyes met. They clearly shared a passion that Molly never had with anyone in her life, including her late husband, and it made her a little sad. No one had missed her while she was gone.

Beth left her with towels and a bar of soap, and Molly stripped off her ruined clothes and sank into the tub. The water was barely warm, but she didn't care. By the time she realized that she hadn't hallucinated seeing Edgar Burgess back in that cellar, that she was really in a steam cab and on her way home, she would have gladly taken a bath in the East River. In full view of the public, if necessary. Anything to wash off the stink and shame that accompanied one when she was held hostage in a steamer trunk by a gang of vampires.

She scrubbed at her skin until it was raw and pink, welcoming the soap's sting over the cuts and scrapes she'd picked up being passed around from monster to monster. Sometimes she was held under their spell. Other times, she'd been wide awake and aware of what was happening to her. She gingerly touched her neck, feeling the raised puncture marks where fangs had pierced her skin. Maybe now the bruises there could finally heal, but she would never be able to wear anything but a high-collared dress or blouse again. She hadn't seen her reflection in a looking glass since the night she was abducted, but she didn't need to see it to know that she looked like something out of a penny dreadful caricature. She could see her body in the shallow water, how much weight she'd lost.

Her ribs were showing for the first time in her life.

She touched her wet hair and cringed. Lord knew how she was going to get all the tangles out of it.

"Ahoy, Beth," said a familiar voice from the corridor. "I got the blood like you asked."

Oh, dear. This could get awkward. "Wait," said Molly. "Give me a minute. Don't come in!" She looked around the kitchen frantically, knowing she didn't have enough time to hop out of the tub, dry off, and get dressed before Edgar opened the door. So she pressed herself against the side of the tub, hooking an arm around the edge, hoping that only her face would be visible should Edgar not hear her.

He cracked it open a hair, but didn't enter the kitchen. "Beth? You in there?"

Molly relaxed a little. Edgar had enough manners not to barge into a closed room. "No, it's me. I'm not ready to receive visitors."

"Ah," he said, understanding in his voice. "Beth takes her baths in there, too. But um, I have some cow's blood, and it should go in the icebox as soon as possible."

Molly shuddered at the thought of drinking cow's blood, but supposed it had to be done. "I'll be out shortly," she said.

"I don't want it to spoil. It's worse going down if it's even close to being warm. Believe me, I know."

Curiosity got the better of Molly. "You've been bitten?"

"A few times. It goes with being a Searcher. But I usually have holy water on me, and that keeps the bites from scarring."

"All right," said Molly.

"All right, what?"

Her stomach turned over, nervousness at the idea of being naked in a man's presence for the first time since her husband's death. "All right, you can come in and put the blood in the icebox." She paused. "Just please cover your eyes first."

It occurred to Molly that she wouldn't ordinarily mind Edgar seeing her naked in the bath if happened under better circumstances. If she wasn't sickly thin, scarred, bruised, and pale, if she didn't feel and look so utterly wretched, she might have welcomed it.

Why hadn't she welcomed it before she was kidnapped? The thought popped into her mind unbidden.

He was quiet for a moment, so long that she thought he might have crept away. "Edgar?" she said.

"I'm right here," he said. His voice sounded odd. "Are you sure about that?"

"Yes," she said. "I'll drink it as soon as I get out of the bath. I just want to get it over with."

The kitchen door opened, and Edgar cautiously stepped in, one hand holding a glass jar of reddish-black blood and the other over his eyes. He kept his body against the wall, sliding along until he reached the icebox. He looked so ridiculous that Molly couldn't keep herself from giggling.

"I'm trying to be a gentleman," he said gruffly.

"I appreciate the effort."

"I'll have to open my eyes to put away the blood without knocking anything over," he said. "I promise I won't peek."

"It's fine. If I didn't look like I'd been a vampire snack for weeks, then I wouldn't even mind."

Molly sucked in a harsh breath. Had she really just said those words?

Edgar froze in front of the icebox, and she guessed he was as shocked as she was. His voice was strained when he replied. "I see. Ah, I'll just put this away then."

Molly's eyes never left him as he stuck the jar in the icebox. His clothes, worn and faded as they were, still fitted him well and hinted at a physique honed by years of hard work and heavy lifting. Constructing dirigible airfields and staking vampires would have that effect on a man, she mused. Her mind flashed back to his lifting her out of that steamer trunk, when she felt the power and strength radiating from him.

Hand over his eyes, he shuffled out of the kitchen. From the other side of the door, he said, "When you're done, I'll need to take your statement for the Searchers."

"I won't be long."

"Take your time."

The bathwater had already gone cold, anyway. Colder, she corrected herself, but it was still better than being filthy and bloody. Molly squeezed it out of her hair and stood up, taking care not to splash it over the tub's sides. She dressed in Beth's borrowed clothes, then on a whim, peeked into the icebox.

Ugh. Just the sight of the jar made her want to vomit. Was it really necessary to drink it?

If a family of vampire hunters said so, then she supposed she must. She sighed, and walked out of the kitchen to find Edgar.

TWO

E dgar paced the length of the parlor, his steps treading over the rag rugs covering the floorboards. He needed to tell Molly what he'd sensed the night she was kidnapped. He'd felt that familiar twinge of pain at his temples that usually signaled a vampire's presence. He'd ignored it, convinced it was just another symptom of the cold he'd been fighting.

He'd been dead wrong, and even though Molly turned up alive, he would never forgive himself. He was certain she wouldn't forgive him, either, once she found out. He would have to go back to adoring her from afar as he always had since she moved into Mrs. Stapleton's boarding house next door.

He glanced at the box resting on the scarred table pushed against the wall. If nothing else, he hoped she would be pleased to see it and her things inside.

Light, feminine footsteps walking along the corridor from the kitchen told him she was out of the tub, sending a whole new wave of embarrassment washing over him. He'd tried to be a gentleman about it, covering his eyes and not peeking. Even though the sounds of her splashing in the water sent images through his head that even he found inappropriate.

Might as well get this over with. "Molly?" he said.

She stepped into the doorway, wearing one of Beth's dresses, hair still damp and unbound. "Yes?"

"Ready for to take that statement?"

She nodded, then took a seat next to him on the couch. He had a notebook in his hand, a pencil poised over it. Taking a deep breath, she described the night she was taken: how she was getting ready for bed, drawing the curtain over her bedroom window, when she spotted a man on the other side. How he had looked straight at her, gaze latching on hers. He had gently suggested that she open the window and invite him in, a notion that felt perfectly logical at the time. "I felt like I was sleepwalking when I left with him," she said, picking at nonexistent lint on her skirt. "I thought I would wake up soon and find myself asleep in my bed, but I didn't... I didn't come out of that state until he locked me in that trunk after he fed from me the first time. He said my blood was the best-tasting he'd ever had." She shuddered. Edgar's heart lurched at the sight as he wrote down her story.

"You said before that he had white hair," he prompted.

"White hair and burn scars on his face and what I could see of his body."

That meant the creature had probably been in a tussle with a vampire hunter or two in his time. Not Edgar, though. He would remember a white-haired vampire. "Thank you. I really appreciate your telling me this. So will the rest of the Searchers."

"I hope one of you finds him," she said vehemently.

"We do, too." Unexpected nervousness had his mouth going dry when he thought about his surprises for her. "I have something else for you." What if his timing was wrong for his surprise? Still, he picked up the box and held it out to her.

She looked at it curiously before taking it from his hands, and the smell of soap wafted from her hair, possibly one of the best scents Edgar had ever encountered.

She lifted the lid, then gave a little cry at what was in the box. "Oh, my goodness!" she said. She looked up at Edgar, tears in her eyes. "You saved all of this?"

"Mrs. Stapleton left all of your things on the sidewalk a few days after you disappeared," Edgar explained, sitting down next to her. "She's evicted people in the past for being late on rent by only a few days. It was mid-morning before I found out, and I saved what I could. Your clothes were taken rather quickly, but there were some other things left lying there that I brought back in case..." He quickly corrected himself. "For *when* you returned."

The remains of Molly's belongings didn't amount to much: a comb, a packet of tortoiseshell hairpins, a couple bundles of letters tied together with ribbons. A small velvet pouch containing a tarnished wedding band and brass locket, the latter holding a tiny photograph of a man Edgar presumed to be her late husband. A couple of embroidered handkerchiefs. A knitted sky-blue shawl that had been mud-stained when Edgar found it, although Beth helped him clean it.

A sniffle escaped her as she dug through the basket, and Edgar's chest constricted. "I didn't mean to make you cry," he said.

"It's all right," she said. "It's just—these are all that's left of my old life now. I'm glad you saved this out of everything, Ed. I mean it." She wiped away tears with one of the handkerchiefs. "It's an odd question, but I don't suppose anyone came around to look for me? Anyone from work?"

Edgar hated to tell her the truth, but he did. "None that I spoke to." Well, aside from Mrs. Stapleton, who was angry about the lack of rent. Her showing up on the Burgesses' doorstep the day after Molly went missing, ranting about what an irresponsible and disrespectful widow she was to have taken off with a strange man during the night, was what tipped him off to start looking for her.

"I assumed as much." She opened the velvet bag and took out the locket. "I suppose you looked at this?"

"I did. I wanted to make sure the hinge still worked." In part to make sure the jewelry was still in good condition, and partly out of curiosity.

She gave him a look he couldn't decipher. "It's fine. I would have done the same thing in your position." She opened the locket, glanced at the picture inside, and snapped it closed. "I've moved on since Kenneth passed, but I'd still prefer to keep reminders of my old life. It shaped who I am now."

Edgar nodded, understanding. "What happened to him, if you don't mind my asking?"

He'd never asked her about her husband, not wanting to intrude, in the years he'd known her. She rarely discussed her old life, only mentioning that she used to live in Manhattan and had worked as a telegraph clerk since her move to Brooklyn.

"He wasn't vampire food, if that's what you're asking," she said. She sighed. "Pneumonia. A perfectly common and very uncomfortable way to die."

Edgar didn't know how to respond to that. "I'm sorry."

She looked away for a moment. "We were married less than two years. He picked up a cough shortly after Christmas and was gone a month later." She tucked the bag back in the basket. "We were just starting out, so we didn't have much money, and I couldn't afford to stay in our flat. I came to Brooklyn and found work at Western Union." She sighed again. "I suppose my job has been filled now."

Edgar had been thinking about that during his trip to the butcher's. "The Searchers may be able to help you," he said. "The New York branch needs clerks for its own telegraph office." He took a deep breath, steeling himself for what he had to tell her next. "Helping you find work is the least I can do for you."

"Why do you say that?" she asked, a hint of alarm in her voice.

He swallowed, dreading having to say his next words. "Because it's my fault you were kidnapped in the first place."

~

MOLLY'S GRIP on the box loosened and it tumbled to the carpet. She didn't move to pick it up, but stared at Edgar in shock instead.

Her words tumbled out of her in a furious whisper. "What do you mean? How is this your fault, Edgar? You could have stopped it?" Her voice rose, and she forced herself to keep from shouting. "*How could you have prevented this?*"

The look on his face was distraught, so miserable and apologetic she almost felt sorry for him. "I thought I had a headache the night you were abducted," he said. "I'd been ill for a couple of days before and I'd had headaches on and off." He ran a hand through his dark russet hair, unable to meet her eyes. "My vampire sense isn't as strong as Ada's or Frank's. I don't always trust it as much as they do. I can't. I just sort of... barge into vampire nests and start staking." He turned beseeching eyes to Molly. "You asked if anyone came looking for you. I was. I've been looking for you since the day after you disappeared. I've killed more vampires over these last weeks than any other Searcher in the state."

He'd been looking for her every night? A little bit of the anger that bubbled inside her cooled. "What about Francis and Beth?" she asked. "They're Searchers too, aren't they? Why didn't they sense the vampire who tricked me into letting him in?"

"They were out the night I was sick," he said. "I didn't know you'd been kidnapped until the next morning, when your landlady said you'd taken off with a man the night before." His voice cracked. "As soon as she said that, I *knew*. I failed you, Molly, and I'm sorry."

More of her anger ebbed a little. "How could you have failed me?" He didn't owe her anything. He was a friendly neighbor, a member of a family of friendly neighbors.

He paused, searching for words. "You've been very special to me since you moved into Mrs. Stapleton's," he said finally. His eyes met hers, and she was surprised to see an uncharacteristic tenderness there. "I wanted to look out for you."

Molly bent over and set the basket upright. "I told you that he tricked me that night."

"Humans can be enthralled. You weren't tricked, and that wasn't your fault."

She shook her head, as if she could rid herself of the memories. That night had been a surreal experience, like a strange dream she couldn't wake up from. She'd felt as if something had taken over her body and compelled her to do things she ordinarily wouldn't. Like open her window and invite a strange man into her room. Like telling him that yes, she would like to take a lovely evening stroll with him. Yes, she could keep looking into his eyes, that wouldn't be a problem. No, she wouldn't scream when he bit her neck…

She blinked and looked back at Edgar. His expression was still utterly contrite, and she could see true remorse in his gaze. It suddenly occurred to her that this was the first time since her kidnapping that she wasn't afraid to look at someone in the eye.

"Thank you for telling me," Molly said. "I can't say I'm delighted you ignored your sense, or whatever you call it, but I appreciate your being upfront about what happened."

He nodded, relief across his face. His shoulders visibly relaxed, as if he had physically let go of tension. "And thank you for saving these," she said. She gathered the dropped items from the floor. "Those are letters my parents wrote to one another before they were married."

"Where are they now?"

"Dead, like everyone else in my life." She allowed herself another moment of self-pity, even though it had been years since her parents' deaths. She stood up. "I suppose I should go drink that blood now, and I should clean the bathtub."

"Don't worry about the tub. I'll take care of it. You have enough to do keeping that down."

He followed her to the kitchen, and she removed the cow's blood from the icebox. "What's the easiest way to do this? You're the expert." She looked at the jar in disgust. "Is this even really necessary?"

"What did the vampires feed you while you were locked up?" he asked. He was dragging the tub across the kitchen floor, taking care not to splash any of the cold, soapy water out the sides.

"Would you like some help with that?" she asked, sidestepping the question about food. She could go for another meal or two, actually, and she wasn't looking forward to drinking cow's blood.

"I can take care of this just fine. Molly, what did they feed you?"

She didn't want to think about being trapped in that trunk, only being pulled out to be passed around among hungry vampires. "Water and whatever scraps they found, when they remembered." She shuddered, recalling the stale bread crusts and slimy meat they tossed her way. She'd been desperate enough to eat it after a couple of days in the cellar.

"So you're underfed *and* missing blood, which means you have to drink this. After you do, I'll see if I can't get some of those bites to heal a little better with holy water." He stopped at the kitchen's back door, meeting her eyes. "If you'll let me."

She wanted every trace of her vampire attacks off her body. If being doused with holy water ensured her scars could be erased, she would take it.

Edgar opened the kitchen door and emptied the bathwater outside, then left the tub beside the jamb. He crossed the room and opened the icebox, removing the jar of blood. "You've done this before?" Molly wanted to be sure he wasn't just trying to get her to go along with something disgusting if it wasn't strictly necessary. Being daubed with holy water? Fine. Drinking cold blood? Ugh.

"I've been bitten countless times and fed from twice. It tastes vile, but it's necessary. Your body only produces so much blood, and it has to be replaced."

"You're *sure* this helps, that I have to do this?" Molly felt her gorge rise at the sight, and she wasn't sure she could do it.

"It's best to just suck it down as fast as you can," Edgar said.

Bile rose in Molly's throat, but she forced it down and unstopped the jar. It was just under three-quarters full, she guessed. Her eyes met Edgar's again, and he nodded encouragingly.

"Maybe try holding your nose," he said.

She hadn't done that since she was a child and her mother forced her to eat boiled cabbage. "All right." She pinched her nostrils shut and raised the jar to her lips.

It was cold and salty, going down her throat in congealed lumps. Molly wanted to gag, and then cry and feel sorry for herself again, but she forced herself to drink it until she only sucked back air. She slammed the jar down on top of the icebox, dizziness overtaking her at what she had just done. Nausea crested over her in a wave as her body threatened to toss it back on the kitchen floor.

Edgar seemed to sense it, because he grasped her elbow and led her to a chair. "Deep breaths," he said. "You don't want it to come back up."

Molly breathed in deep, cleansing lungfuls of air until her nausea had mostly passed. "That was impressive," said Edgar. "I've seen Searchers suck back less blood than that and still be sick."

"Save your accolades," said Molly. She closed her eyes. *Breathe in, breathe out.* "It may come back up yet."

"Accolades?"

"Congratulations," she said by way of explanation.

"I'll have to remember that," he said. "I like that word."

She kept breathing deeply, willing the cow's blood to stay where it should. "What am I going to do after this?" The question slipped out without her thinking about it twice. But she had to know: she was without a home and a position. The Burgess family was of the same limited means as herself, and there were more of them, besides.

He knew what she meant. "Work for the Searchers, if you want. You're an experienced telegraph operator, and the New York branch needs one. It's even better if you're a good speller, because God knows none of us are. You can stay with us as long as you need to. You can take Ada's room until she gets back."

"The Searchers are lacking someone with good spelling skills? How do you know I'm good at spelling?" she asked, still breathing through her nose.

"Hell, you know the word 'accolades' and use it

in an ordinary sentence. That puts you miles ahead of everyone else running the telegraph."

She laughed a little, some of her nausea dissipating. Maybe she wouldn't be sick, after all. "Will I have to drink more blood?"

"It depends on what the doctor says."

A doctor. Wonderful. But Molly supposed it was necessary. "Does he work for the Searchers, too?"

"He does. And I still have to make that report."

Almost on cue, a key scraped in the heavy brass lock on the front door and it swung open on squeaking hinges. Francis Burgess's voice shouted a hello, followed by a quieter male voice that Molly didn't recognize. The doctor, she supposed.

Edgar stood up, holding out his hand, and it took Molly a second to realize that he was helping her up.

She smiled, her eyes meeting his, and laid her palm in his hand. She was struck by how warm and alive he was, and by her own reaction to him. Her body prickled with awareness, and with it, a corresponding warmth. She didn't want to look away, but it wasn't because a vampire's thrall compelled her not to.

Agate had been the first person to touch her since Kenneth died. No, not a person, she reminded herself. A monster. The memory of his cold, dead hands gripping her shoulders as his teeth sank into her flesh was as indelible as an ink stain on cloth.

But so was Edgar's touch and his dark eyes fixed on hers, and there was nothing but strength and kindness there. And, Molly thought, something more.

But his next words were all business. "Let me find some holy water before Helford examines you."

~

By early afternoon, Edgar had written his report, and Molly was examined by Dr. Helford, the Searchers' long-serving physician. Edgar returned to the butcher shop for another jar of blood while she was looked over, just in case Helford recommended more. Besides, it never hurt to have some blood on hand when one was a vampire hunter.

He stopped at a small curio shop near the butcher's on his way home. It was a tiny space, dimly lit, crammed with clockwork toys, baubles, periodicals, jewelry, and cheap bouquets held together with yellowed lengths of lace. The scent of tobacco permeated the air. He often picked up adventure magazines there. They were usually the closest to literature the Burgess family read, and was pleased to see the current issue of *Murray's*. He tucked a copy under his arm and carefully inspected the rest of the shop's wares. Funny that he never really looked at anything but the magazines before.

A present. He could pick something out for Molly. He had just enough money on him until his next payment from the Searchers to buy her something nice. He hoped so, anyway; a dingy shelf held out an assortment of cheap gold-painted jewelry that was already tarnished that he didn't think she would like. The things her landlady tossed out in the street were delicate and beautifully made.

He finally picked out a couple of the dime

novels his sister was fond of, and a bouquet of daisies, the only fresh bunch on offer. The lace that held it together was fastened with a small brass pin shaped like a beetle whose wings opened when it was wound up. An uncharacteristic nervousness swept through Edgar at the thought of presenting Molly with his gifts and wouldn't go away.

Dr. Helford was still at the house when he returned, his medical bag over one arm and hat in hand. "How is Mrs. McKillip?" Edgar asked him by way of greeting.

"I told her and your sister-in-law that she should take some more blood over the next two days," the physician said. "She also needs to eat some more and put some weight back on. But otherwise, for someone who was held captive by vampires for over two weeks, she's doing quite well." He nodded toward the bag holding Edgar's purchases and the bouquet in his hand. "I trust you stopped at the butcher shop?"

"He thinks I've gone mad since I've been there twice today for cow's blood, but I did."

"Have her take a cup of it tomorrow, and another the day after that. If her condition worsens, and I don't expect it will, let me know." He put his hat on and said his goodbye.

After leaving the blood in the icebox, he found Molly in the house's small parlor, sitting on the couch. She looked more serene than she had before he left for the butcher shop, and he guessed the Helford had been upfront as usual about her good prognosis. The early afternoon sunlight reflected bright gold off her blonde hair, now tied back in a serviceable knot at the nape of her neck. She was, and always had been to Edgar, absolutely lovely.

"Dr. Helford says you're on your way to recovery," Edgar said.

"Hearing that from a physician takes a great deal of care off my shoulders." She spied the bouquet and books in his hands. "What's that?"

Feeling like an awkward schoolboy in front of the first girl he'd ever been infatuated with, Edgar held out the bouquet. "These are for you."

Surprise lit up her features, and her lips turned up in a smile. "Thank you. This is a pleasant surprise."

He held out the books. "Ada's fond of these. She says reading something ridiculous helps the soul."

She took them from him and examined the cheap blue paper covers. "You can never go wrong with giving me a novel. Thank you for the books, too."

An unexpected relief flowed through Edgar at her pronouncement. She picked up on it, because she asked, "Were you worried I wouldn't like them?"

"Yes." He sank into the couch next to her. Weariness tugged at him, another reminder that he'd hardly slept these last weeks.

She shrugged and leafed through one of the books. "All I was allowed to read when I was in school was the Bible and etiquette guides." She held up the bouquet and sniffed the daisies, then unpinned the tiny brass beetle from its lacy perch. She sat down next to him and wound it up, letting it crawl across her skirts. "I will never turn down an opportunity to read something fun."

Edgar couldn't offer an opinion on that, having left school at twelve, the same as Francis. Ada had continued her studies a little longer, wanting to be an airship pilot at one point, but eventually caved in to the Searchers' requests and joined their ranks. He was grateful that their parents had insisted all of their children be literate, though. Knowing how to read and write made going through life much easier, despite his not being an expert at it.

He pushed all thoughts of education away. He was suddenly very aware of her presence, the smell of her soap filling his nostrils, the heat from her body setting all of his nerve endings on fire.

"Why did you give me all of this, Ed?" she asked.

Ah, the question he both wanted to answer and feared to. Because he wanted to tell her it was because he loved her, that he blamed himself for her abduction, that he knew there was nothing he could do to make up for what had happened.

"It's an apology," he said.

"You've already apologized, and I told you it wasn't necessary."

Before he could talk himself out of it, Edgar blurted out, "I love you, Molly."

She immediately stiffened next to him, and the beetle crawled off her skirts and dropped to the floor. The parlor was so silent he could hear her shallow breaths and the tinny scratch of the mechanical insect's legs. But he wasn't going to speak the next words; those were up to her. There wasn't any way to expand on what he just said.

"What?" Molly's voice was a hoarse whisper, an edge of panic in it.

"I have the highest kill count in the city right now because I've been looking for you," he said.

"That doesn't explain your saying you love me."

"It does. I never stopped searching." His eyes

met hers, and he saw the shock reflected there. "I've been in love with you for a long time. It killed me when you went missing and I knew I could have done something to stop it."

"You were sick, Ed…"

He cut her off. "I still should have investigated."

She stood up, the bouquet in one hand and the books clenched in the other. "Edgar, I know you have good intentions, but I cannot handle this right now. Between the vampires and this infatuation you seem to have…" She shook her head and looked away. "I need to be alone for a while."

She hurried out of the parlor and Edgar listened to her footsteps as she ascended the stairs to Ada's bedroom. He remained rooted in place, unable to follow her.

A few moments passed and Edgar kept staring out the parlor window, at the sun-drenched street. Francis strolled in. "I thought I'd give you a minute."

"I suppose you heard everything."

Francis threw himself into a chair, long legs sprawled across the threadbare carpet. "You're an idiot and your timing is terrible."

Edgar wanted to lick his wounds in private. "Shouldn't you be sleeping? Don't you have a shift with the Searchers tonight?" he asked irritably.

"I begged off and picked up a shift tomorrow night at Coney Island Airfield instead. You really should stop by. They're guessing the whole thing will be finished by the beginning of August and there goes the work."

"I know." Did he ever. Money was always tight for the Burgesses, but with Edgar taking on as much work with the Searchers as he had, he'd certainly been short of it more than usual. Airfield construction work was paid in cash daily, and that cash was significantly more than the pittance offered by the Searchers.

"I came here to bother you about the airfield construction, and I did that."

"Then you can probably leave."

"Nah, I'd rather tell you how badly you fucked up telling Molly that you love her."

Edgar stood up. "Not now."

"She's right, you know. Dropping that on her the day she's pulled out of a vampire den is a lot. You should have waited a few days, at least. Months, preferably, if ever."

"I'm leaving now."

"I hope you're going to the airfield to sign up for a shift. They're short of afternoon and night workers."

It wasn't a bad idea. "Fine, I'll go to the airfield."

MOLLY SAT on the edge of Ada's bed, unable to move. Her breath came fast, like she was about to start crying, and her heart thundered against her ribs. She was briefly reminded of how much Agate had liked feeding from her when she was terrified, that he liked feeling her pulse vibrate. Tears spilled down her cheeks, and she wiped at her eyes with her hands.

Edgar's bouquet rested on top of the chest of drawers in the corner, the dime novels beside it. A small bookcase full of similar paperbacks was beside the chest, giving credence to Edgar's claim about Ada's choices in reading material. Molly liked Ada. She had never seemed to be afraid of anything, a fearlessness confirmed by the revelation that she was a vampire hunter. For a few seconds, she wished that Edgar's sister was home and could offer her some advice. Molly was two years older, but at twenty-five Ada had a worldliness and wisdom about her that Molly didn't. She knew now that it had to come from a culture of monster hunting.

It wasn't that Molly didn't *like* Edgar. Quite the opposite. He was always polite and cursed far less than Francis or Ada did. She'd always found him attractive, with his russet-colored hair that shone in the light and his powerful forearms that were revealed when he rolled up his shirtsleeves, which was often. Hearing his confession in the parlor was as almost much of a shock as seeing Agate at her window the night she was kidnapped.

Why did he have to tell her *now*? Why not in a few days, when she had some time to absorb everything that had happened?

And why did she have to be such a ninny about it? It took a great deal of courage to tell someone that, and she threw it back in his face. She didn't know who to be angrier with, herself or Edgar.

Was he expecting her to return his affections? Molly stood up and paced the small room, footsteps muffled by the large, colorful rag rug covering the floor. She liked Edgar very much and considered him and the Burgess family among her few friends in Brooklyn. She had finished grieving for Kenneth a long time ago and moved on, something she and her late husband discussed well before he fell ill. They had both agreed long ago that if one of them passed away too young, the other would go on with life. They didn't have enough money to stay single forever.

Of course, when Molly started to feel comfortable in her rebuilt life, she ended up snatched by a vampire.

She plucked her handkerchief from the basket of things Edgar had saved from the street and wiped her eyes. Poking through the basket, she couldn't help but be amazed that he'd known exactly what to save for her. Her clothing could be replaced, but her mother's hairpins couldn't, nor could her letters. The handkerchiefs her aunt embroidered for her were irreplaceable, too.

She sat back down on the bed, letting herself feel the exhaustion of the last weeks pour over her. Even though it was only early afternoon, she was ready for sleep.

And why shouldn't I sleep? Kenneth always said that sleeping during the day was a way to avoid one's problems, and until now Molly agreed. But Kenneth hadn't known about vampires or that his wife would end up tricked by one. He wouldn't have known that she would be locked in a trunk for days at a time and find herself guzzling blood after her rescue.

She hadn't truly slept in weeks. Taking a rest for a few hours wouldn't hurt.

Molly unlaced her borrowed boots and lay back on the bed facing the window, welcoming the warm sunlight filtered through the curtains. It was a welcome sight. When she had been locked away in that cellar, she thought she might never see the sun again. But it was difficult to remember how much she had missed it when she thought about Edgar's declaration. She didn't want to be dependent on him and his family while she sorted out her conflicting feelings for him.

As she dozed off, she thought only one thing in her life was certain right now: she had to leave the Burgess home as soon as possible.

THREE

The ever-present threat of tears pressed behind Molly's eyes, held at bay by sheer willpower alone. Beth still sent an occasional sympathetic glance her way every few moments as they jostled about the steam cab's backseat. While it was a trifle cleaner than the one that brought Molly to the Burgess house, it was cramped. Molly's borrowed satchel rested between them, holding all of her things while she fled from Edgar.

Not just Edgar, she silently amended. She looked out the grimy window at the passing cityscape, of people strolling along sidewalks, the displays in shop windows. She was fleeing her own complex feelings, too, unable to process his confession while in his presence.

His declaration echoed in her mind, and with it, her own shocked reaction. In another time, when she hadn't known about the existence of vampires and she was still an ordinary Western Union clerk, she might have welcomed it. If there had been a chance of the two of them connecting in a normal courtship, she would have enthusiastically agreed to it. But she *did* know about vampires, and there was no chance of a normal courtship, not when one person in a couple routinely put his life on the line to battle bloodsucking monsters.

She sighed, then spoke for the first time since Beth hailed the steam cab. "You're certain your friend won't mind me staying with her for a while?"

"Of course not. Violet keeps a spare room in her flat for just these kinds of occasions. She's a gracious hostess." Beth reached over and squeezed Molly's hand reassuringly. "And remember that we meant it when we said that could get you a position with the telegraph office. The New York branch is in desperate need of someone with your skills."

Someone good at spelling, Molly recalled. Was she expected to correct Seachers' errors when they sent off their cables? When she'd started off at Western Union, she tried to gently point out spelling errors and was rebuffed for her efforts. It was easier to say nothing. Or perhaps Edgar was only trying to be nice.

Violet Singer turned out to have a beautiful flat in a gracious old building, a space larger than the Burgess home. She also had a head of shining silver hair, carefully gathered into a bun at the nape of her neck, a contrast to her youthful face. Fine dark brows knit themselves together in concern as she greeted Molly, despite the warm smile on her face. "I received your message," she said to Beth. "This is Mrs. McKillip?"

Beth nodded. "Yes, she's our next door neighbor and needs a spot to stay for awhile."

"I have just the place." Violet turned to Molly. "Welcome, Mrs. McKillip."

"Please call me Molly."

"And you must call me Violet." She eyed Molly's bag. "You travel light."

"I don't have a lot."

"There's plenty of space for in my guest room anyway. Let me get you settled, and then we can sit down and chat, if you like. Or take a nap, the bed's comfortable. I also have a bookshelf you're free to borrow from."

Molly thought about the paperbacks Edgar had given her that were now packed away in her bag. "Thank you."

"Are you going to be all right if I leave?" Beth asked.

"It's broad daylight, so I can already tell that Violet isn't a vampire. I'll be fine." Molly dropped her bag to the hardwood floor. Impulsively, she threw her arms around Beth, who fiercely hugged her back. "Thank you for your help," she whispered. A few of the tears that had been threatening behind her eyes spilled over.

"Of course. We're friends. This is what friends do for each other. Violet is one, too."

Molly had herself collected when Beth left the flat, leaving her and Violet alone. "Beth didn't go into too many details, and I'm not going to pry," Violet began, but Molly cut her off.

"Edgar blames himself for me being kidnapped and I don't, but he told me he loved me and I can't handle that." Molly's words came out in a rush.

Violet raised a brow. "I see."

"What did Beth and Frank tell you?"

"Frank came over earlier today to ask if you could stay with me for a while, until you've sorted things out for yourself. Of course, I said yes. A friend of the Burgesses is a friend of mine. His exact words were, 'Edgar is a fucking idiot' but didn't go into specifics otherwise." She inclined her head to a carpeted corridor. "Let me show you to your room."

Molly followed her through the flat to a beautifully appointed bedroom. She could hardly notice it for the words she needed to get out. "I don't know if he's an idiot, but he does have terrible timing." Molly realized she needed to talk about this, get another perspective that wasn't Edgar's brother or sister-in-law. "He told me he loves me."

"Hm." Violet sank into the rocking chair in the corner of the room and gestured for Molly to sit. She did so on the edge of the bed. "I take it this wasn't news you wanted to hear?"

Molly was quiet for a moment, thinking about Violet's question. She had been mulling over similar ones on the ride over to the flat. It wasn't bad that Edgar was in love with her. She would have been interested in exploring a relationship with him had he made any indications to those feelings, at least in another lifetime where she wasn't recovering from being a vampire meal for weeks. She liked him a great deal, more than she should. "I don't know if it wasn't something I didn't want to hear," she said slowly. She fixed her gaze on the coverlet's embroidered pattern, threads twisted together to resemble vines. "I wasn't ready for it. I wasn't expecting it. The timing was very poor. And further, what was I supposed to do knowing that? Am I obligated to give him a chance?"

Violet's reply was firm. "Of course not."

"Not to mention, I was dependent on him and his family after he pulled me out of the trunk. I still am, since they've arranged for me to have a job with your organization. I didn't have a lot before I was lured out of my room, but it was still mine. I'd found a job on my own, found a place to live. I valued my independence, meager as it was."

"You aren't obligated to take the job with the Searchers, either. I'm certain Western Union would hire you back," Violet replied.

Molly shook her head. "No, they won't. Not after I disappeared without a word for weeks. No one would take an employee back under those circumstances." She held back from asking if Violet had ever had a job outside of working for a secret vampire hunting society.

"If you don't want to work for the Searchers, I can help you find work elsewhere. Whatever you want to do, how you want to do it, I can help."

Molly thought about the sumptuous flat Violet owned, about her fine clothes that definitely weren't automaton-produced ready-mades, and wondered where her money came from. She had no doubt that Violet had the means to help her restart her life, as loathe as she was to accept more help. All she could think to say was, "Thank you."

Violet's expression softened. "I hope I'm not too forward when I say this, but I hope we can be friends."

Molly nodded, forcing herself to meet Violet's eyes. "I hope so, too." She looked away, this time focusing on an oil painting of an unfamiliar landscape on the opposite wall. "If you don't mind my asking, are you married? Do you live alone?"

For a few seconds, Violet looked a little flustered. Just as quickly, she composed herself. "No. This line of work doesn't bode well for marriage, I'm afraid. We're secretive about our work. We have to be. Could you imagine the chaos if the population at large found out that vampires are real? Romantic entanglements are all but impossible with people who aren't aware of the Searchers, if not a member themselves."

Realization dawned on Molly at Violet's answer. "Do you suppose that's why Edgar never said a word to me before today? Because he couldn't?"

Violet gave a tiny shrug in response. "It's possible."

"What about Beth and Frank? Both of them are dhampir descended, too, aren't they? They would've known about the Searchers their entire lives."

"They were childhood sweethearts."

Molly shifted, then smoothed out her skirt. "I'll be damned."

Violet tilted her head, a quizzical expression on her face as she waited for Molly to elaborate.

"Ed's timing is still terrible. I wish he hadn't sprung out with love declarations when he did, but it's done and over with." Molly stood and crossed the distance to the bedroom window. Outside was a typical New York spring day scene of people bustling about, the road lined with steam cabs and horse-drawn carriages. And likely not a single person strolling along the sidewalk knew that beneath the streets and hidden away in attics were monsters sleeping the day away. "I now understand why he didn't say anything before." She turned back to Violet.

"You aren't obligated," she began, but Molly cut her off.

"I know I'm not obligated to do anything for him. All of this is going to take some time to get used to, and I have to heal physically. I just..." Molly searched for her next words. "I just don't feel so overwhelmed by Ed saying what he did. I get it now."

Violet smiled. Molly was unexpectedly speechless by the sight. With her silver hair and youthful face, she looked like what Molly imagined a fairy godmother must appear. She was striking. "Take as much time as you need. Stay here as long as you want. I'll enjoy having company. If you would still like to take a position in our telegraph office, it's open to you as well. Just say the word."

Molly nodded. Something inside her unknotted itself, tension radiating away. It would take far longer to recover from her experience with vampires, but she would get there, eventually. She could let someone else help her as she restarted her life under a new normal, a person who was aware of and survived an encounter with monsters. "I think I will," she said. "When and where do I start?"

FOUR

The Searchers' Brooklyn-based headquarters was housed in a nondescript brownstone in a neighborhood nicer than where the Burgesses lived, but not by much. The house and the ones on either side of it were owned by the Singers, one of the oldest in American vampire hunting history. The only indication that the house wasn't completely ordinary were the blackened silver strips hammered around the door to ward off vampires, intentionally kept tarnished to evade thieves.

It was nearing twilight when Edgar strode through its front door. The scent of garlic was in the air, the result of bulbs hanging behind window transoms and doorways. He was there to pick up his much-needed pay, and then he was off to take an overnight shift at the Coney Island Airfield. He was used to staying up all night, and besides, night shift work paid a little better.

There was another reason for his trip to headquarters tonight: Molly was now gainfully employed by the vampire hunters as a telegraph operator, working the afternoon to evening shifts. She had stayed out of his way since his foolish declaration nearly a week ago, having moved in with Violet Singer and taken an advance on her wages according to Beth.

He still wasn't sure what he would say if he saw her here tonight. Part of him wanted to apologize, not for his feelings but for his terrible timing. Another baser part of him wanted to ask if there was any chance at all for a future together. He was nearing thirty; it was past time to settle down and he wanted to do that with Molly. But he knew neither was likely to be a good idea.

He had another gift for her this time as well, only it was more practical than romantic. He checked his pocket again and was reassured to feel its smooth surface. He should have given that to her instead of the flowers the day he pulled her out of Agate's hideaway.

The Searchers' headquarters was illuminated by a mishmash of gas lamps and flickering electric lights, the beginning of a much-needed modernization effort. It was slow-going, Edgar noted, given the pittance vampire hunting paid and the need for more modern communication methods rather than light fixtures. Installing a modest telegraph office on-site —in secrecy, no less—had been a better investment.

Edgar picked up his wages and made his way to the communications room, heart pounding furiously against his ribcage. What if Molly wasn't there, and he'd fretted for nothing? What if she *was* there? What if…

His thoughts ground to a screeching halt when he walked in. Hunched over a stack of telegraph slips at a scarred wooden desk, pencil in hand, was Molly, who paid no notice of him.

Edgar quietly cleared his throat. She started and looked up, green eyes wide.

Both seemed to be struck speechless. Edgar broke the silence. "Hello."

It took a few more seconds for her to form a response. "I'd ask what you're doing here, but…" She looked around the room.

"I work here," he said, and immediately felt like an idiot.

She offered him a small smile. "I know. Are you working tonight?"

"At the airfield. Overnight pay is time and a half." He summoned his courage and removed his gift from his pocket. "I brought you something." Seeing her expression shift, he hastily continued. "It's practical."

"For me, books are practical. I enjoyed the ones you gave me, by the way." A blush touched her cheeks.

He relaxed a little. "So is this." He held out the small silver crucifix to her.

"More jewelry?" She raised her eyebrow, and only then did Edgar notice the small brass clockwork beetle pinned to her bodice.

Well, *that* was an encouraging sign.

"Vampires are sensitive to silver and crosses," he said by way of explanation.

"Even if I was baptized Episcopalian and haven't set foot in a church since my wedding day?"

"I can count on both hands the number of times I've been in a Catholic church since I was baptized. I'm long overdue for confession. It's the *faith* behind the power of holy objects over evil that repels vampires, not religion itself. If that wasn't the case, I'd be dead several times over by now."

She accepted the cross from him, protectively curling her fingers around it. "Thank you."

Her gaze held his for a moment. "Do I need anything else? A stake and mallet, maybe? Violet suggested it."

"She's a vampire hunter. She's being practical, too. Telegraph operators don't need them."

Molly flinched slightly as if she realized she'd just brought up her new flatmate. Her voice softened. She looked away for a few heart-stopping seconds before she spoke again. "Ed, I didn't move in with Violet because I'm mad at you. You and your family have been nothing but kind to me since I was kidnapped. *Before* I was kidnapped," she quickly added.

He stared at her, knowing that disbelief had to be written across his face, but didn't offer a verbal response.

"I wasn't prepared to hear what you said, and I didn't know how to respond. I needed some space, but I didn't intend to hurt you. I like you very much, Ed."

Hope flared in Edgar's chest, strong and bright. Even so, he said, "My timing was still terrible."

"It was," she agreed. "Don't do that again. This is a lot to take in on its own without that kind of declaration." She gestured around the room with ink-stained fingertips. Other than the telegraph paraphernalia, the room was filled with overstuffed bookcases, stacks of crudely carved stakes, and extra bottles of holy water. A couch was draped with overcoats and gloves, the origins of which were a mystery to Edgar.

That same hope cautiously returned. He nodded, trying to keep his expression neutral.

"I think I need a little time," she said. "Is it unfair to ask you to wait for me?"

"Yes!" Realizing his mistake, he added, "No, I mean. It isn't unfair to ask me to wait. I'll do that. Won't be a problem."

She stood up and dusted imaginary lint off her clothes, a dress Edgar recognized as once belonging to Beth. She left a silvery streak of pencil lead across her skirt but didn't pay it any mind. She walked around the desk, stopping when she was a few inches from Edgar.

His pulse beat rapidly as the smell of her soap and beneath it, her skin overwhelmed his senses. She leaned in and brushed her lips over his cheek.

Edgar fought against every impulse he had that told him to kiss her back, to brand her with his own scent, but he stayed still. She'd asked him to wait for her, and he would.

Still, he allowed himself to take her hands in his own. "What's next?" he asked.

She bit her lip. "I suppose someday we could take the streetcar to Central Park sometime, take a walk, and then share a meal. It's what respectable couples do."

Edgar wasn't sure he would ever fall into the category of respectable, but Molly did. "What about a hot air balloon trip? The Academy of Flight and the Aviation Authority is hosting a festival next week."

"Also a respectable activity." She moved away from him, and he immediately missed the contact. "I'll see you soon, Edgar."

∽

After having had a few days to stew over her troubles, Molly felt a little less discomfited about Edgar's confession. As she tidied her desk for the evening after he left headquarters, she could even admit to being intrigued. More than that, she thought. As she'd told him when he stopped by, she liked him. She respected Edgar, and always felt the same from him. He was someone she could rely on.

And he would always be one of the most attractive men she'd ever met, an opinion she held since the day she met him. Taller than she was, but then most men were, broad-shouldered, with a thick mop of dark russet hair she always wanted to run her fingers through.

It was half-past ten when she left the Searchers' headquarters, and it was only a short walk to the flat she now shared with Violet. Her flatmate would be out hunting tonight, although she said earlier in the day that she didn't expect to see too many vampires. The problem in Brooklyn was mostly under control for the time being, according to her. The Searchers were focused on tracking down the oldest and most elusive vampires, like Agate.

Molly couldn't help but shudder a little at the thought of him. "Where do they get these names?" she mumbled to herself as she walked along the street. The evening air was brisk for May, and she was glad she'd brought a shawl borrowed from Violet with her.

She reached into her pocket and felt the crucifix there, reassured by the tiny object. While Brooklyn's streets were still busy enough so she wasn't terribly worried about being snatched by a vampire again, she still kept herself on the lookout for anything suspicious.

As if you would know what to look for. Agate had looked like a perfectly ordinary man, albeit an exceptionally pale one with nearly white hair who dressed in black like he was in mourning, when he could be bothered to put on clothes. He'd appeared at her bedroom window the night he took her, eyes fixed on hers as she got ready for bed. But the oddity of that had been flung from her mind as his thrall took hold. She gritted her teeth, trying to force away the memory.

The streetlights shining over Brooklyn blotted out any stars, but they paled in comparison to the eerie light of the moon hanging overhead. She paused, transfixed at the sight. The moon looked to be nearly red, and for half a second she thought it looked ill. What was it her father called it? A blood moon. A lunar eclipse, she would discover as an adult, but blood moon sounded so much creepier. She vaguely recalled looking at one with her parents one night. She had been allowed to stay up late to see it. The moon had looked almost grotesque then, and it did now, especially in light of the new things she had to be afraid of. She no longer felt ridiculous for being twenty-seven years old and still wary of the dark. There was good reason to be.

She sighed and continued walking. At least there were still people about at this late hour. She wondered what Edgar was up to at the airfield. She paused, not responding when someone bumped into her and muttered an insult her way.

She'd told him that a walk in the park would be a nice way to start their relationship. It wouldn't exactly be respectable to be wandering around a construction site in the middle of the night, but Molly could go there, perhaps share supper with him. Or whatever the meal was called when it was eaten in the middle of the night.

Smiling to herself, she hailed a passing steam cab, a plan forming in her mind.

MOLLY RARELY HAD reason to travel to Coney Island. As she walked around, she remembered why she avoided it. It was noisy as all get-out even at night, and parts of the midway were still open. Why anyone would want to strap themselves into the ramshackle rides and place their lives in the hands of strangers, she didn't know, and she wasn't keen to research it personally.

The airfield construction area was nearly half a mile from the amusement park itself, and a small, steam-powered train shuttled people back and forth. No one paid any attention to her as she boarded. She noticed a few other women onboard as well, some carrying lunch pails. She relaxed a fraction. Maybe it wouldn't be unusual for her to show up with a meal for her and Edgar.

A few shacks had been built on the construc-tion site, selling food and coffee that Molly could smell as soon as the train stopped. Torches offered enough light to see workers' faces, and Molly was surprised to see more than a few women donned in coveralls, helping to carry heavy wood planks and tools. She should be able to find Edgar. She hadn't thought about how she would before she made her impromptu journey.

A mustachioed man wearing a New York Avia-tion Authority uniform stopped her before she could make her way to the construction zone. "You lost?"

His accent was pure Brooklyn, expression friendly despite his brusque greeting, and Molly smiled. "I'm looking for someone."

"Which division?"

She shook her head. "I don't know. His name is Edgar Burgess."

"Burgess, yeah. I know him. He's stuck on pipes." Before Molly could ask where that was or move, he said, "Wait by that stand. You can't go to pipes wearing those shoes. I'll get him." He thumbed in the direction of a food stand. "Who's looking for him?"

"Mrs. McKillip."

"I'll bring him to you."

"Thank you." She walked to the shack, took a seat at a rickety wooden table, and waited. It was too dark to re-read one of the dime novels Edgar had given her, now stowed in her satchel, so she watched the construction site's bustle. A massive wooden platform had been constructed about a hundred yards away and was crawling with people.

Molly spied a familiar russet-haired man walking toward her about a quarter of an hour later, surprise across his features. She stood up, surprised to feel her heart swell at the sight.

"You're a sight for sore eyes," Edgar said.

Her heart fluttered, and it took a few seconds for her to find her voice. "Hello to you, too."

"What are you doing here?" he asked. "Not that I'm complaining, but nighttime construction sites aren't the safest places for a lady."

"I wanted to see you," she said. "I thought we could maybe have supper together." She looked at the shack behind her. She sucked in a deep breath, suddenly nervous. "The point is I wanted to see you." She exhaled, looked around the muddy construction site, and continued. "I don't think I thought this through, though. You're clearly busy."

His brows lifted in surprise. "I can stop for supper. And I'll see you home after this. It isn't wise to be wandering around in the middle of the night."

She nodded, and knew he wasn't talking about pickpockets. Besides, her kidnapping perfectly showed why she wasn't always safe inside, either. Even though her new home had silver strips hammered into the windowsills and Violet insisted on keeping garlic bulbs nailed to the inside of the front door as they were at the Searchers' headquarters, Molly still wasn't totally assured of her complete safety.

The shack behind them served grilled fish hauled in from Sheepshead Bay, and Molly paid for two giant pieces wrapped in newspaper over Edgar's protests. They sat at one of the rows of tables filled with workers, the noise offered by voices and clanking machinery loud enough so they had to shout to be heard.

"Two hours!" he said. "I'll walk you home then."

She smiled. "I look forward to it!"

IT WAS JUST after two in the morning when Edgar was able to leave the construction site. Being assigned to pipes was backbreaking work, but it paid the best, and Edgar did well enough that the foreman didn't mind his early departure.

He stopped and looked back at the team's handiwork before walking back across the site to where Molly waited. Working on pipes could mean assembling the massive structures that would transport steam throughout the airfield, or it could refer to sanitation; he'd been working on the former tonight. His arms and back ached from the exertion, but he welcomed it. It meant he'd put in a decent night's work, and it was nice to have one that didn't involve staking the undead for once.

Molly was where he told her to wait, inside one of the makeshift food stands. The electric lighting was spotty and flickered enough to irritate Edgar, but bright enough so anyone coming in or out could be clearly seen. He hadn't sensed any vampires in the vicinity of the airfield construction, since it was too crowded for them to hunt, but that didn't mean one of the dumber ones wouldn't try to make a snack out of someone at any point. It never failed to be cautious.

Speaking of cautious… Edgar dearly hoped they wouldn't run into a vampire tonight; he'd left his stake and mallet at home. One of the foremen could easily find them and that would only open the door to questions Edgar wasn't allowed to answer. He still managed to conceal a short length of scrap wood and quickly sharpen it into a point before he left the site to meet Molly, who took his arm as they walked away from the site to a stand where ornithopters for hire waited. "Do you want to fly back to the mainland? It'll be faster," he said.

"That sounds lovely, thank you."

An ornithopter pilot spotted their approach, bowed, and held open the door to his conveyance's passenger basket. "Looking for a ride?"

Edgar nodded. "Just to the Brooklyn airfield."

"I can do that. Hop in." He smiled, revealing a mouth with a missing tooth, then pulled down a pair of comically oversized flight goggles from the top of his head. Edgar and Molly stepped inside the basket. The pilot took his seat at the controls. "Hang on."

They obeyed, gripping the sides as the ornithopter made a choppy ascent.

A sharp ache suddenly sprang to his temples, distinctive as a drumbeat. *Damn it!*

He looked up, but the sky was cloudless and devoid of starlight, empty of everything save the red moon. "Ed?" Molly asked, worry in her voice. "What's wrong?"

Once upon a time—hell, even a couple of weeks ago—Edgar would have lied and said everything was fine, that he must have heard a dirigible overhead or some other stupid excuse, but not now. Not with Molly.

"There's a vampire nearby," he said, his voice a stage whisper.

Molly gripped his arm tighter and turned wide, terrified eyes to him. "Where? Is it the pilot?"

"Not onboard," he said. The pain was gone, which meant the vampire was, too. He looked up. "Flying. Some of them can take the form of a bat."

She turned terrified eyes to him. "What? Why didn't you tell me that?"

"I didn't think to," he said, feeling like an idiot. "There aren't as many old vampires in New York as there are elsewhere. But yes, some of the older ones can shapeshift." He closed his hand over her wrist, eyes fixed on hers. "I promised you I would keep you safe and I mean it. As soon as the ferry docks, I'll take you home."

"Violet's out for the night," she said. He saw a film of tears mist her eyes in the dim light offered by the ferry's lanterns, and she swallowed. "I don't want to be alone tonight, Ed."

"Then you can come home with me." He searched the sky again, but didn't see or sense anything. The vampire was gone.

She slumped against the side of the basket, relief across her features and in her voice. "All right. I'd like that."

Despite the danger that might await them when they landed or while they walked along the street, Edgar's body prickled with awareness at the suggestion in her voice. Was it suggestion? Or was he a lovesick idiot who misinterpreted everything she said?

But she'd come to the construction site tonight to see him, he reminded himself. She said she was amenable to a personal relationship, and he knew she wasn't talking about being platonic friends. Would it be so wrong to read something more into her words?

Cautiously, he held out his arm to her. She leaned into him, wrapping hers around his middle. "Thank you," she said into his chest.

OF COURSE, it would be their luck that there wasn't an available steam cab to be found at the Brooklyn airfield once they landed. "Damn," Edgar said. He took Molly's hand and they quickly moved away from the crowd to the street. She was easily able to keep up with his pace, and even though he'd promised to keep her safe, she couldn't help but feel a little nervous as the crowds thinned out. Brooklyn at half-past two in the morning was a scary place.

"We'll just walk until we find a cab," he said. "Steam or horse, I don't care."

"Aren't horses sleeping this time of night?" She tried to keep her voice light, but she could feel the tension radiating through him where his skin touched her gloves, could feel his strength. In that instant, she realized he was just as much of a predator as a vampire was.

"I'm sure some of them are awake." He paused and looked around. A gas streetlight extinguished itself, darkening the curb they stood on.

"Molly," he said. A chill slithered down her spine at the quiet urgency there. "There is a chapel across the road, and the doors should be open. They always are. Go there and wait for me." He removed a small stake from his trouser pocket.

A shrill, inhuman noise cut through the night air. Molly looked up, and in the dim light from the other gas lamps saw a flying black shape.

Sensing her hesitancy, Edgar gave her a small push and snapped, "Go! Run, damn it! I'll come get you in a few minutes!"

Black wings flapped way too close to Molly's face for her liking, and she couldn't help but shriek. But she obeyed, and bolted across the street to a small structure whose sign read *Brooklyn Episcopalian Automatic Chapel, All Are Welcome!* The church's wooden doors easily opened with a heavy creak, and she slipped inside. She leaned against the door and tried to catch her breath. "You'd better come back for me," she said quietly, a catch in her voice.

The church's vestibule was dimly lit by a gas lamp turned low. The light barely concealed the scuffed wooden floor and balding carpet runner. Molly listened closely but didn't hear anything but the pounding of her heart in her ears. "Hello?" she said.

No one replied. Unease left goosebumps popping up along her skin.

Shouldn't there be a minister in a church? Molly padded the carpet length until she stepped into what passed as the chapel's nave. Flameless candles threw sputtering, dull yellow light across the scarred wooden pews. An elaborately sculpted brass cross was fixed to the far wall, and beneath it on a small raised platform was a phonograph, bolted to a pulpit. An engraving on the pulpit read *Please Turn On Phonograph For Prayer of Eternal Salvation.*

There wasn't a clergyman here, Molly realized. She looked up at the church's small stained windows, unable to see what was going on outside. Should she return to the street and help Edgar? She looked around the chapel for something she could use as a weapon, but all she saw were stacks of religious tracts and a few copies of the New Testament. A table on the left, draped with a purple velvet cloth, held tiny bottles of clear fluid. A handwritten card in front of them read *Holy water! Please help yourself!* Really, did people baptize their children in an automated chapel?

Well, the holy water could be helpful. If Edgar was bitten…

Molly shuddered. She didn't want to think of such a thing. Having her bites cleaned with it hurt far more than she expected.

The creak of the front door had her scrambling for cover, but before she could dive under a pew, she heard Edgar's voice. "Molly? Are you here?"

Her heart leaped at the sound, and she ran

back to the vestibule to see Edgar. Without thinking further, she launched herself at him, and his arms automatically locked around her waist, lifting her up.

Then his lips were on hers, teasing her own apart. Molly forgot all about vampires as her tongue tangled with his, enjoying their first kiss. Her hands slid over his shoulders to his neck, but sticky wetness on his skin had her pulling away. "Ed?" she said. "What's that?"

He let her go abruptly, as if remembering something important. "The bastard got a few bites in there," he said. A wave of nausea swept over Molly as she remembered her own bites. "I don't suppose there's any holy water in here."

She grabbed his hand and led him farther into the chapel. "You're in luck, or at least as much luck as someone bitten by a vampire can be. There's holy water free for the taking."

Edgar sat down heavily in one of the pews as Molly picked up one of the small bottles, wincing in pain. He pulled a handkerchief out of his trousers pocket and handed it to her. Saturating it, she asked, "Is there anything special I have to do to make this work better?" The bite was small, on the spot where his neck met his shoulder, and still bleeding. It didn't look too horrible, certainly not the big bite wounds Molly had been subjected to, but it wasn't as though she was an expert in vampire behavior yet.

"Just hope it's actually been blessed by a clergyman and isn't there for show… *fuck!*" The epithet bounced off the small chapel's walls as Molly pressed the handkerchief to his neck. "That answers that question. Give a man some warning next time, would you?"

"I guess it's been blessed, then. And I feel like we shouldn't be swearing in church."

Something thudded hard against a stained glass window. Molly looked up as a vague black shape slammed itself against the window again. "Ed? Did you stake that vampire?"

"No, he's still out there." He winced as Molly daubed holy water on the bite. "Vampires can't enter consecrated buildings, even if they're invited in. My new plan is to hide out here until morning, and then take you home."

"But the vampire…"

"Will still be out later, and I'll find him then. Right now, we're safe." His eyes fixed on hers, and Molly swallowed at the intensity reflected there. She couldn't remember the last time she'd been kissed like that, even if it had to be interrupted by his injury.

"Do you have any other bites?" she asked, trying to keep her voice from shaking.

"Just scratches." He held up his wrists, where thin ribbons of blood were already drying in reddish-brown streaks. "These shouldn't be as bad as the bite." Still, he cringed when Molly applied the holy water-soaked handkerchief to the wounds.

She pressed it to the bite again. "Hold this," she said, then sat down next to him and lifted her skirt enough to reveal stockings and petticoat. In a moment of self-consciousness, she was glad that the church's light was dim enough so he wasn't likely to see how worn out and darned her underclothes were.

"Molly?" There was a teasing lilt to his voice.

"Give me a minute." She pulled at her petticoat until she tore a strip of thin cotton away, then straightened her skirt. "I don't have anything else to use as a bandage."

"Good thinking."

She lifted away the handkerchief and wrapped the makeshift bandage around his neck. "Can you get the pin from my dress? I need something to hold this in place."

His eyes lifted a fraction, but he reached for the brass beetle pinned to her bodice. Her skin felt hot at his touch even through her layers of clothing, but it was over too soon as he unfastened the jewelry. She pinned the bandage in place with shaking fingers.

"Now what?" she asked. "Do we just sit here?"

A thump from the bat against the window was her reply. She sighed.

"That was an older vampire, so he may be able to stay awake until just past dawn," Edgar explained. "I still don't think it would be a bad idea to stay here for a little while."

Would they be there all night? "I'm sorry for all of this," she said.

"Why?"

"Because if I hadn't come out to the construction site tonight, you wouldn't have left early and we wouldn't have run into a vampire. And if you had, you would have had time to stake it without worrying about me."

"I don't always get vampires on the first try, Molly. This wasn't your fault." He laced his fingers through hers. "Remember when I said I'd always protect you? This is part of that."

Once again, Molly was struck by how warm and alive he was, and by how much she missed having contact with another person. The kiss

Edgar branded her with when he burst into the church was still on her mind.

"I meant what I said back at home."

She knew what he was referring to, but that strange fear she felt when he confessed his feelings for her was gone. Hearing those words had been a sensory overload for her that day, but now that she had some time to process what had happened, now understood her own feelings for Edgar—she was all right with this. And she wanted more than kisses from him.

"I'm glad you told me," she said. "I meant what I said at headquarters, too." He paused, as if waiting for a reaction from her. She didn't know how to respond. Was he expecting an "I love you" in return? She didn't know yet if she was ready to say those words.

But she wanted a future with him, even if it would be fraught with worry as he kept hunting vampires. She wanted that chance to rebuild her life with him at her side.

Another slam of the bat's body against the window had both of them whipping their heads in its direction. "He doesn't give up, does he?" Molly asked. "He must really hate you."

"I held a cross to his face when he bit me, so I'm not surprised he's angry. Do you still have yours?"

She plucked the small cross he'd given her from her pocket. "Right here."

"That's my girl."

Molly felt herself flush with pleasure at that, and with it, a wave of desire rolled over her for the first time in years. Before she could talk herself out of it, she leaned over and kissed him, needing to recapture the feeling he left her with when he burst into the church's vestibule. Needing to reassure herself that he would be all right.

Edgar responded immediately, tugging her into his lap. His hands roved up her body to cup her face, his fingers outlining the shape of her cheekbones and lips like he was reading a map. His touch was feather-light, but it may as well have been a brand for the effect it had on her. She closed her eyes against the onslaught of sensation, wanting more of his hands on her body but still almost overwhelmed by her senses going into overload for the first time in years. She leaned into him, forehead touching his, relishing the contact. Then she pressed her mouth to his, needing to confirm if her reaction to him kissing her in the vestibule wasn't merely a fluke.

It wasn't. Something primal in her flared to life, and she knew Edgar felt it, too. She ran her fingers through his hair, gripping it in her hands as she always wanted to do, as if she was afraid to let him go.

She was. She was afraid for him, for the monster that waited for them outside the church. She knew he would never give up hunting them, even though he was paid next to nothing, even though he and the rest of the Searchers could never receive any kind of recognition for what they did to keep the world safe. Being with Edgar Burgess would mean always having that constant worry at the back of her mind when he left to hunt. He could come home with worse wounds than he suffered tonight. He *would* come home with them, Molly knew.

But she realized she was all right with all of this. Edgar was a good man; she'd known that since she met him. Everything he'd ever said, the way he behaved toward her and others all pointed to a man who could be depended on, who would never stop searching to save someone he loved. Molly had been waiting for someone like him all her life.

His tongue found the sensitive spot under her ear, teasing a gasp out of her. His low chuckle sounded in her ear, and one of his hands slid along her thigh, down to her bent leg, up under her skirt. His fingers trailed up her stockinged leg, coaxing another harsh breath from her, and his hand stilled on her knee. His eyes met hers, silently asking permission.

"Don't stop," she whispered.

His questing fingers continued sliding up her leg, gliding over the sensitive skin of her inner thigh. Molly's breath halted in her throat as he pushed aside the loose fabric of her drawers to her damp center. He slid a finger inside her, moving it in and out in a maddening rhythm that would never be enough to satisfy her. A strangled mewl escaped her throat, and Edgar fitted another finger into her. His pace increased and Molly's body moved with it, riding his hand. His thumb brushed against her clit, a tiny movement that had her nearly thrashing against him.

Her nipples scraped uncomfortably against her clothes, and all she could think of was getting out of them to cool down her overheated body, and getting Edgar out of his, too. Her fingers fumbled at his clothes, but with his free hand he grabbed hers that was plucking at his trousers placket.

"Not here," he said. "This is for you."

She could feel the hot, hard length of him through his pants and even in her lust-hazed state could tell he was just as aroused as she was. "Why not?" His fingers pumped in and out of her, nearly obliterating all rational thought.

"Because I've already waited two years," he said. "I can wait a little longer to do this properly."

The idea was so ridiculous that Molly would have laughed had Edgar not moved his thumb in circles over her already sensitized flesh as his fingers still pumped into her. "But this…" She swallowed the words *isn't proper* as the first wave of climax washed over her, not that it mattered anymore. All that did right now was Edgar. Her eyes closed of their own will and a sob escaped her.

Edgar increased his pace. "Come for me, Molly." His voice was hoarse with desire, but still commanding, and Molly had no choice but to obey.

She came apart on Edgar's hand, her cry swallowed by his mouth on hers. She sagged against him, totally spent, and he pulled his hand out from under her skirt. She made no attempt to right herself, content to straddle his body and never leave.

His own breath was ragged in her ear and his cock still pressed against her. She reached down between their bodies and stroked him through his pants, eliciting a sharp hiss from him. "Not here," he said again.

"But what about…?"

He cut her off. "Later, I promise. In a bedroom with a door that locks so we can get naked and do this right." He moved her hand away, lacing his fingers through hers. "Besides, my vampire sense won't let up. That could be a distraction."

Heat suffused Molly's face at his reminder the church's doors were kept unlocked, but she wouldn't let herself feel embarrassed. She framed Edgar's face in her hands and kissed him in a wordless thank you. "Can you tell if it's just the one vampire out there?"

"Just the one for now. I can handle him with some holy water."

Both of them jumped as a man's voice crackled across the chapel. "Oh heavenly Father, who hast filled the world with beauty, open our eyes to behold thy gracious hand in all thy works…"

Molly shrieked and lifted herself off Edgar's lap. He bent over, shoulders shaking, and she realized he was laughing as the voice continued speaking. In the next instant, she looked at the phonograph that had begun to play a scheduled recording, and she relaxed a little. "Is there any way to switch that off?" she asked.

"Search me."

"Oh God, the creator and preserver of all mankind!" the voice said, rising in volume. "We humbly beseech thee for all sorts and conditions of men!"

"Conditions, of course," Edgar said, running a hand through his hair. "You know, I really don't understand Episcopalians."

"It's reciting the Book of Common Prayer. I think it'll be talking for a while." Molly pressed a hand to her chest, willing her heart to slow down to a normal tempo.

"I think I'd rather take my chances outside trying to stake the vampire that listen to that," Edgar said. As if on cue, the bat slapped itself against the window again. "That must be stinging him a bit, at least as much as my head hurts right now. He's a determined bastard." Catching Molly's disapproving look, he added, "What? If we can do what we just did in a chapel pew and not have hellfire come raining down on either of us, I doubt the man in the sky will care if I say 'bastard' in what's really a bastardized version of a church."

When he put it that way... Molly nodded. He had a point.

Edgar plucked a watch from his pocket and checked the time. When he spoke, his voice was lower, almost a stage whisper. "It's a quarter past three. I'd like to stake that vampire now that I have some holy water at hand and have rested a bit. It'll make things easier." He picked up his makeshift stake from the pew, then tucked a couple of the small bottles of holy water in his pocket. "Stay here. I'll be back in a few minutes."

The warm, lazy sense of happiness Molly let herself feel in the aftermath of her shattering apart in his arms evaporated. "Ed," she said, wariness in her voice.

He silenced her with a kiss. "I do this for a living, Molly. This part of Brooklyn never really sleeps. What if he eats someone while I spent the night cowering away in here? I'd never forgive myself." His expression softened as he held up his stake, as if to prove his point. "There's only one out there. I can deal with him. I'll be back soon."

Molly knew she would never win this, and in a way, she didn't want to. Edgar was a hero. He would always do what was right. "Please be careful," she said.

"I will. I have something to look forward to, remember?"

The reminder, and the look of promise in his eyes, sent another wave of heat through her. "All right."

She walked with him to the vestibule, pausing in front of the wooden doors. "I love you," he said.

She brushed her hand over his cheek.

He didn't seem to care about a response in kind. "I'll come back in one piece." With one final kiss, he opened the door and stepped into the night. Outside the chapel, the moon glowed a sickly red.

CHAPTER

FIVE

The spring air was cool, a sharp contrast to the warmer air of the automatic chapel behind him. But Edgar welcomed the change; it heightened his senses. Senses which were telling him that a vampire was very close. With his stake in hand, he looked around the darkened street, trying to pinpoint the monster's exact location.

A snarl alerted him to the vampire's presence. A very pale, naked man swooped in front of him. In the dim light offered through the church's windows, he could see ugly scars crisscrossing his face and body, the results of being splashed with holy water. *What's one more?* Edgar thought. He thumbed the lid off one of the small bottles and flung it at the monster.

It hit the vampire in the face. He screamed, a high-pitched, keening sound that set Edgar's teeth on edge and probably awakened half the neighborhood. Hopefully, they had the sense to stay in their beds. The holy water assault distracted the vampire long enough for Edgar to leap on him, stake in hand, and knock him to the ground. They tussled for a moment, the vampire's strength returning de-

73

spite the agony the holy water had to be causing him. The smell of burning, undead flesh assaulted Edgar's nostrils. He desperately wanted to gag, but he couldn't allow himself such a distraction. He tried to aim his stake at the vampire, but the monster's grip on his wrist was more of a hindrance than he expected.

Edgar dug his knee into the vampire's stomach, distracting him enough to gain the upper hand again. The vampire fell to the ground, hissing, fangs gleaming in the church light. Edgar raised his stake, but the vampire leapt to his feet again, quickly scrubbing at his ruined face. Chunks of skin rolled off and drifted to the street to disintegrate into ash, one of the more disgusting things Edgar had seen lately.

Edgar quickly unstopped another bottle of holy water and threw it in the vampire's direction, this time splashing his naked chest. The motion tore another scream from the monster, but he still advanced on Edgar.

Light spilled on to the street as the church's doors opened, and Molly's enraged yelp had both Edgar and the vampire looking in her direction. "Agate!"

This was the vampire that had held Molly in that cellar? Fresh rage flowed through Edgar. He threw himself at the naked vampire, knocking him back down to the ground. He looked up to see Molly's shadow move as she ran into the fray. "Get back in!" he ordered.

"No!"

Something heavy, wrapped in her shawl, came crashing down on Agate's skull, inches from Edgar's own head. It wasn't enough to kill the vampire, but it stunned him enough so Edgar could sink his stake into his chest. Edgar leapt up just as the vampire's remains crumbled into dust.

He turned to Molly, who still held the shawl-wrapped thing in her hand. Shock was written across her face. "He's really dead this time?"

"Yes," Edgar said. "Molly, what were you thinking?"

"I heard screaming."

"That was the vampire!" Now that the immediate danger had passed, and Edgar couldn't sense any other vampires in their vicinity, indignation swamped him. "You could have been killed!"

"So could you!"

Well, that was a possibility; it always was in his line of work. "All right," he said, conceding. "That doesn't excuse your doing something incredibly dangerous."

"What did you expect me to do? Just sit there? I can't do that anymore."

She wasn't afraid anymore, he realized.

He wrapped an arm around her, bringing her closer to him. "No, I don't suppose you can," he said. "It's hard to sit by and do nothing when you *know* there are these horrible things wandering the night and what they can do." He looked at her weapon. "What's that?"

She extricated herself from Edgar's hold and unwrapped the weapon. "There was a stopped clock in the vestibule," she said, handing it to him. His hand sagged with its unexpected heft. It was indeed a heavy brass clock, weighing about eight or ten pounds. He wound it up, setting the hands to the correct time.

"Impressive, and a good choice of weapon." He kissed her temple. "But don't ever do that again."

Molly returned the clock to the church's vestibule, and they walked into the street. "Now what?" she said.

A steam cab clattered along the street, the first one they'd seen in hours. Edgar led her to the curb and waved at the driver to stop it. "We go home," he said.

~

THEY RETURNED to the Burgess family home, creeping up the stairs so as not to wake Francis and Beth. Edgar paused outside his bedroom door, as if he thought Molly might be having second thoughts. "Are you sure?" he whispered.

The suggestion in his voice was unmistakable. "More than I've ever been," she said.

He opened the door and switched on a flameless lamp, revealing a spartan, uncluttered space that was the opposite of the organized chaos of his sister Ada's chamber. Molly eased the door shut behind them, unsure of how to proceed. On the one hand, it had been a long night for both of them; on the other, she wasn't the least bit tired yet.

Judging from the way Edgar's eyes roved over her, he was thinking along the same lines she was.

"You'll stay the night here?" he asked.

"It's a bit late for me to be changing my mind."

"If you did, you could sleep in Ada's room."

He was offering her a way out, letting her know she didn't have to do anything she didn't want to. It was sweet of him, but unnecessary. That brief distraction in the automatic chapel was just a tease; it hadn't been nearly enough.

She wanted Edgar Burgess every way she could get him. "I'm staying," she said firmly. Emboldened by those words, she reached for the buttons that marched down the front of her dress, flicking them apart. Edgar sucked in a harsh breath. "Aren't you going to help? My getting undressed is a bigger production than yours is."

He crossed the room in half a second and had her shrugging out of her dress almost as quickly. He bent down to unlace her boots, tossing them aside in front of the closed door. He ran his thumb along her sensitive insole, prompting a squeak from Molly, who had always been a little ticklish. Her response drew a promising look from Edgar.

His hand rested on her calf, sliding up the back of her knee. "May I?"

Molly's senses were on fire from those simple, light touches. His hand skimmed up her leg, under her chemise, to the top of her stocking and slowly peeled it down, then the other one.

He rose to his feet, taking in the sight of her in the dim light offered by the flameless candles. Under his scrutiny, she felt her nipples stiffen and dampness between her thighs. She noticed his breath becoming more ragged and his hands shook when they reached for her. His lips touched the side of her neck, near one of her newly acquired scars, and kissed it like it wasn't the ugliest thing in the world.

Maybe it wasn't. She certainly didn't feel ugly when she was with him.

"Wait," she said.

He immediately stilled. "Molly?" he said against her neck.

She ran her hands over his shirt. "You're wearing too many clothes."

He relaxed against her and clasped her hip, plucking at her chemise. "So are you." But he quickly unbuttoned his shirt and tossed it to the floor. He was all lean muscle as she'd always suspected, healed scars crisscrossing his body from old bites. He was the most delectable man Molly had ever laid eyes on.

He took her face in his hands, now a gesture she would always associate with him, and kissed her. Then he led her a little closer to the bed in the middle of the room. "I've dreamed of this dozens of times," he said. His fingertips lightly touched her face, as if he was committing her features to memory. "Molly…"

"I'm here, Ed," she said. "I'm not leaving. You don't have to flatter me." Too late, she realized how that comment might be construed, and she opened her mouth to clarify what she meant.

But that earned a soft chuckle from Edgar. "It's not flattery," he said. "And how I feel about you isn't strictly physical." Molly looked down at the bulge in his trousers, then back at him wordlessly, suppressing a smile. "All right, part of it's physical. But you're so much more than that." He stilled. "I started looking for you as soon as I found out you were missing. I knew you were out there, still alive."

"And if I hadn't been? What if Agate had turned me into one of them?" It was a question that had lingered in the back of her mind since he lifted her out of that trunk.

"I don't know what I would have done." Edgar leaned his forehead against hers and brought her hands to his bare chest. "I hoped I wouldn't have to find out, and I can't tell you how relieved I was to know I never had to make that decision."

They both knew what he referred to, and Molly was again grateful that Edgar found her when he did. What *if* she had been turned against her will? It didn't bear thinking about, especially not now. She'd survived, and that was what mattered.

Those thoughts flew from her mind when he kissed her again, teasing her lips apart. His body pressed against hers, erection heavy against her hip, and she felt her own center throb in response. She stepped away from him long enough to pull her chemise over her head and let it drift to the floor. She stood before him, totally naked. She couldn't help but preen a little at Edgar's widened eyes.

"What do you think?" she asked.

He swallowed. "That this is better than I thought it would be."

She sat down on the edge of the bed. "We haven't even started yet."

Those words were all that was needed to galvanize Edgar into action. He crossed the short distance between them and pushed her back on to the bed, his body covering hers. The fabric of his pants was rough against Molly's skin, his skin hot against hers. She reached between their bodies and fumbled for the placket on his trousers. This time Edgar let her and helped her push them down his hips. She wrapped her hand around his cock, eliciting a sharp hiss of pleasure from him.

He moved her hand away. "If you keep doing that, it's going to be over before it starts." He nipped at her neck, then breathed a hot trail down her throat to her breast, taking one stiff nipple in his mouth. Molly gasped, back arching, as his hand teased her other breast.

"Ed," she said, not bothering to hide the urgency in her voice. The memory of the church was too strong to ignore right now when he was here. She needed so much more.

Her legs fell apart and he nestled between them, shaft hot against her thigh. It nudged against her entrance and she clung tighter to Edgar, urging him to continue. He did, with agonizing slowness, drawing out a frustrated moan from her, until he was fully seated inside her.

She locked her ankles around his back as he started to move. His thrusts started off slow but sure, stoking a fire that had been building inside her for hours. He laced his fingers through hers, pinning them above her head into the mattress, and lightly bit at her neck, a passionate gesture that didn't revile her as she thought it might. Instead, it set her senses aflame, and she moved her hips in tempo to his body.

Already she could feel her orgasm growing, and Edgar seemed to sense that. He shifted his body a few degrees, changing his angle just enough to bring her closer to the edge, hips meeting hers. The motions teased a whimper from her throat, and that was all the encouragement Edgar needed. He increased his pace and Molly felt herself come apart. His mouth covered hers to muffle her cry, and a few seconds later he pulled out of her, hand working his cock. He spilled onto the blanket, his breath loud and heavy in the room.

Molly lay back in a boneless heap, totally wrung out. Edgar pushed the soiled blanket off the bed and lay back next to her, draping a clean bedsheet over them. He tucked her into his arms and she leaned her head against his chest.

He dropped a kiss to her forehead. "You're amazing," he said.

She giggled and snuggled in closer to him.

"I meant every word I've ever said to you," he said. "I love you, Molly."

This time, the words didn't fill her with panic. And when she thought about it, they didn't the first time he said them, either. She'd been exhausted and frightened after her ordeal with the vampires, physically ill from drinking animal blood to replace her own, and had never considered before then that she might have found love again. She never allowed herself to think of it. Molly McKillip had always done everything right, including widowhood, to the point of putting aside her own hopes and happiness.

Edgar forced her to look outside those restrictions, and thank God for that. His saving her was more than just a rescue from vampires.

She levered herself up on an elbow to get a better look at him. "Ed," she said, "That's good, because I love you, too."

His dark eyes met hers, nothing but tenderness there in the flickering light offered by the candles. She settled back against him. "Marry me," he said.

The words sent a little thrill through her, but they were still unexpected. "What?"

"I'm serious, Molly. I want to marry you. Whenever you say so."

She slid an arm across his chest, all the more to get closer to him. "Yes."

SIX

Edgar hated that he and Molly kept getting stalled by the thick crowds at the New York City Airfield. The sun still shone brightly at a quarter past six on the evening of May thirtieth, providing a glowing backdrop for the vessels landing and departing. Ada's dirigible had docked fifteen minutes prior, and she had to be getting impatient waiting for them. He held on to Molly's hand as they finally approached the dock where the German-built dirigible rested and scanned the faces around them, looking for his sister and her mysterious new beau.

People were everywhere. Edgar hated this particular airfield and its constant bustle, and wished its Brooklyn counterpart accepted international flights.

"Ed! Over here!"

Before he could respond, a pile of russet-colored hair tickled his nose as his sister wrapped him in a hug. He squeezed back, surprised at how much he'd missed her, and swallowed back a lump that had formed in his throat.

"I missed you," Ada said. "I missed everyone so much."

"We missed you, too." He planted a kiss on the top of her head.

Ada pulled away from him and regarded Molly, her dark eyes mischievous. Edgar dearly hoped that she wasn't about to embarrass him. "He finally told you," she said, and hugged Molly. "Welcome to the family."

Well, it could have been worse.

Ada stepped back and placed a hand on the arm of a tall, well-dressed man with sandy hair and blue eyes. "Edgar, Molly, this is Maximilian Sterling," she said, pride in her voice. "He's a writer and honorary Searcher, soon to be a real one. Max, this is my brother, Edgar Burgess, and our neighbor that he's been in love with for years, Molly McKillip."

There was that charming younger sister commentary, after all. Edgar held out his hand. "Pleased to meet you."

"You as well." Maximilian Sterling had a firm handshake and an unmistakable high class English accent. Now that Edgar could get a good look at him and Ada, he saw his sister was better turned out than she had been before she left for Dresden. Even his unpracticed eye could tell that her dress wasn't an automaton-produced readymade. But she wore the same bright, easy smile she always did, and her hair was still a wild, curly mess. She was still Adaline Burgess, dhampir-descended vampire hunter from Brooklyn.

"Max writes the Captain Reed stories we like," Ada said.

That raised his opinion of Max Sterling a little higher. "Welcome to the family as well, then."

"I'm relieved to hear that. I was somewhat worried that you and your brother might be waiting to kill me."

"I already told you, Max, we don't do that in America," Ada said. To Edgar, she said, "You received my letters and cables? Frank and Beth are expecting us?"

Edgar nodded. "They're excited to see you." They were also looking forward to telling Ada about her being an aunt in a few months, but he didn't mention that. "We won't be staying at the house much longer," he said, with a look at Molly.

Ada arched a brow and crossed her arms over her chest, an expression so much like their late mother when she was irritated. "Why would that be?"

"We're getting married," Edgar said.

Ada shrieked, a noise that drew the attention of passersby and made Edgar and Max wince. She threw her arms around Molly. "Oh, my God, that's wonderful! When?"

"In the summer." They hadn't picked a date just yet. "We've already found a flat closer to the Searcher headquarters." Ada let go of Molly long enough to squeeze Edgar with a strength that belied her smaller size. "Oof! My ribs, Ada!"

Ada let him go. "I beg your pardon for being happy that you're finally settling down."

This time, it was Edgar's turn to arch an eyebrow at his sister. "You're doing the same."

The adoring look Max and Ada shared was unmistakable, and without looking back at Edgar, she said, "I suppose I am."

Shadows fell over the airfield as another, smaller dirigible prepared to land alongside the larger German vessel. They all looked up. "I think we should leave," she said. "It's about to get much more crowded here, and I can't see any porters, anyway."

"We don't have much," Ada said. She held her much-loved satchel that Edgar knew would contain few personal effects, including the stake and mallet she never traveled without. Max had also packed lightly, judging by his own bag similar to Ada's, albeit newer.

Molly linked her arm through Edgar's. "Let's find a steam cab."

Max and Ada walked alongside them. "They're nicer than the ones in Paris," Ada told Max. "But dirtier than London's or Bern's. It isn't a long trip, anyway."

"That isn't saying a great deal as to their cleanliness," Max said.

But Molly wasn't paying attention to their chatter. "You really meant it when you said you wanted to be married in the summer?" she said, her voice a whisper.

"I did. I meant every word I've ever said to you. What about the sixth of July? We could honeymoon in Niagara Falls."

"Is Niagara Falls vampire-free?"

"I don't know. I'll still bring my stake and mallet. It's the smart thing to do."

Her hand tightened around his arm. "I like the sound of that."

The four of them made their way over to a stand of idling steam cabs, and walked to the front of the line. Edgar held open the rear doors for Molly, Ada, and Max. He gave the driver the Burgess family address, then slid in after them. "So you just set your wedding date?" Ada said.

She didn't miss much. "Yes," Edgar replied.

"Has anyone in this family ever *not* been impulsive?" she said. Despite her words, she smiled at Max and squeezed his hand.

"I don't think so," Edgar said.

Molly laughed. "I hope not."

Something clanked in the steam cab, and it lurched into motion, taking them through Brooklyn's familiar streets, back to their home.

About the Author

Jessica Marting is a sci-fi and paranormal romance author, art enthusiast (not quite an artist, despite all that time in art school), an avid reader, and makeup collector. She lives in Toronto.

Sign up for her newsletter at jessicamarting.com/newsletter for pre-order alerts, sales, freebies, and more.

ALSO BY JESSICA MARTING

Magic & Mechanicals

Wolf's Lady

Sea Change

Bound in Blood

Dragon's Keep

Spellbound

The Searchers

Blood Ties

Blood Moon

Blood Virtue

Zone Cyborgs

Haven

Paradise

Oasis

Safe Harbor

Sanctuary

Refuge

The Commons

Supernova

Celestial Chaos

Standalone Novels & Novellas

Spindle's End

Trade Secrets

Neon Vice

Dead Ringer

Rapture

Escape From Europa 10

Castaways

Demon's Favor

Her Perfect Match